W9-ARL-643

Jake headed down the stairs. Ally watched him go until he disappeared around the corner of the house.

Then she closed the door and turned from it, catching the faintly lingering scent of his cologne.

And even though she didn't understand why, she couldn't resist breathing it in.

Breathing it in and picturing Jake all over again.

Jake standing at the door, facing her, towering above her in all his broad-shouldered, masculine majesty.

Looking into her eyes.

Touching her cheek.

Jake in a position from which he could easily have kissed her...

She yanked herself back to reality.

Kissed her?

Jake Fox?

Maybe she should have *her* head examined, too!

Dear Reader,

The sometimes rocky relationship between a mother and daughter is at the heart of this story. Ally and Estelle Rogers have had a rough history that's evolved into chilly, formal civility. But when the aging Estelle's health becomes a concern, Ally finds herself in the position of needing to step in. Not an easy task when Estelle lives in Chicago, and Ally has a thriving design business in sunny Los Angeles.

But Jake Fox—the sexy, headstrong psychiatrist who has befriended Estelle—is more than willing to lend Ally a hand along the way. And while he's at it, a little something starts up between Jake and Ally that has nothing at all to do with family obligations—and everything to do with the primal heat they can't help but generate every time they're alone together....

As always, happy reading!

Victoria Pade

DESIGNS ON
THE DOCTOR

VICTORIA PADE

SPECIAL EDITION®

Published by Silhouette Books

America's Publisher of Contemporary Romance

If you purchased this book without a cover you should be aware
that this book is stolen property. It was reported as "unsold and
destroyed" to the publisher, and neither the author nor the
publisher has received any payment for this "stripped book."

Special thanks and acknowledgment to Victoria Pade for
her contribution to the BACK IN BUSINESS miniseries.

 SILHOUETTE BOOKS

ISBN-13: 978-0-373-24915-2
ISBN-10:   0-373-24915-2

DESIGNS ON THE DOCTOR

Copyright © 2008 by Harlequin Books S.A.

All rights reserved. Except for use in any review, the reproduction
or utilization of this work in whole or in part in any form by any
electronic, mechanical or other means, now known or hereafter
invented, including xerography, photocopying and recording, or in
any information storage or retrieval system, is forbidden without
the written permission of the editorial office, Silhouette Books,
233 Broadway, New York, NY 10279 U.S.A.

This is a work of fiction. Names, characters, places and incidents are
either the product of the author's imagination or are used fictitiously, and
any resemblance to actual persons, living or dead, business establishments,
events or locales is entirely coincidental.

This edition published by arrangement with Harlequin Books S.A.

® and TM are trademarks of Harlequin Books S.A., used under license.
Trademarks indicated with ® are registered in the United States Patent
and Trademark Office, the Canadian Trade Marks Office and in other
countries.

Visit Silhouette Books at www.eHarlequin.com

Printed in U.S.A.

Books by Victoria Pade

Silhouette Special Edition

Breaking Every Rule #402
Divine Decadence #473
Shades and Shadows #502
Shelter from the Storm #527
Twice Shy #558
Something Special #600
Out on a Limb #629
The Right Time #689
Over Easy #710
Amazing Gracie #752
Hello Again #778
Unmarried with Children #852
**Cowboy's Kin* #923
*Baby My Baby #946
**Cowboy's Kiss* #970
Mom for Hire #1057
**Cowboy's Lady* #1106
**Cowboy's Love* #1159
**The Cowboy's Ideal Wife* #1185
*Baby Love #1249
**Cowboy's Caress* #1311
**The Cowboy's Gift-Wrapped Bride* #1365
**Cowboy's Baby* #1389
*Baby Be Mine #1431
**On Pins and Needles* #1443
Willow in Bloom #1490
†*Her Baby Secret* #1503
†*Maybe My Baby* #1515
†*The Baby Surprise* #1544
His Pretend Fiancée #1564

***Babies in the Bargain* #1623
**Wedding Willies #1628
***Having the Bachelor's Baby* #1658
The Pregnancy Project #1711
‡*The Baby Deal* #1742
***Celebrity Bachelor* #1760
***Back in the Bachelor's Arms* #1771
***It Takes a Family* #1783
Hometown Cinderella #1804
Bachelor No More #1849
§*A Family for the Holidays* #1861
The Doctor Next Door #1883
††*Designs on the Doctor* #1915

Silhouette Books

World's Most Eligible Bachelors
Wyoming Wrangler

Montana Mavericks
The Marriage Bargain

The Coltons
From Boss to Bridegroom

*A Ranching Family
†Baby Times Three
**Northbridge Nuptials
††Back in Business
‡Family Business
§Montana Mavericks:
   Striking it Rich

VICTORIA PADE

is a native of Colorado, where she continues to live and work. Her passion—besides writing—is chocolate, which she indulges in frequently and in every form. She loves romance novels and romantic movies—the more lighthearted the better—but she likes a good, juicy mystery now and then, too.

Chapter One

Ally Rogers felt shell-shocked as she stared out the window of the Chicago-bound airplane.

It wasn't every day that some stranger told her there was a situation with her mother that she needed to "get to Chicago—immediately—to deal with."

It wasn't every day that some stranger told her that even though Ally might not want to be involved in her mother's life he wasn't giving her the option *not* to be any longer.

It definitely wasn't every day. It was just yesterday.

This week had been hellish for Ally right from the start. As a well-known interior designer dealing with celebrity clients, she sometimes had to travel the world to get to their sprawling mansions, and she was frequently required to keep odd hours to accommodate her clients' hectic schedules.

Yesterday had been a prime example of that. She'd flown in from Italy at dawn, catching only a few hours sleep on the plane. Then she'd had to rush home, shower and change her clothes before dashing to meet with a national news anchor while he did his live morning show. During his commercial breaks she'd presented pictures of what was being implemented by her design team in his Tuscan villa and gotten the okay on her plans for the rest of the project.

Ignoring the jet lag she was suffering, she'd had a full twelve hours of other appointments and details that had had to be attended to before she'd finally gotten back home again. Where a curt voice mail from a Jake Fox had awaited her. The name wasn't familiar to her and he hadn't said more than that to identify himself, only that he needed to speak to her ASAP about her mother. That it was an emergency.

When Ally had heard that, she'd wanted to kick herself for not having given her mother her new cellphone number yet. But Ally had been en route to Italy on Sunday when she would have made her weekly call to Estelle. And to be honest, she'd just been so busy that she'd forgotten all about it.

The moment she'd heard Dr. Fox's message, she'd dialed the number he'd left. And if his message had been curt and impatient, it was nothing compared to her conversation with him.

After the under-his-breath "It's about time" response to her call, Ally had said, "Are you with my mother now? Who are *you?*"

"A friend of Estelle's from the senior center," he'd said. "If you talked to your mother more often you'd know that."

"Are you her doctor?"

"No, I'm not her medical doctor, but Estelle needs to *get* to her doctor. Unfortunately her friends and I can't persuade her to do that. Besides, this is a family situation, something a stranger shouldn't need to tell you," he'd added, under his breath again. Then he'd proceeded, in a more matter-of-fact tone, to say that Estelle had been unwell, that it wasn't exactly clear what was going on with her, but that he was convinced she needed medical attention.

After trying and failing to get more out of the doctor—who insisted he had no more information to share—Ally had instantly dialed her mother's house. But there hadn't been any answer. She didn't have the numbers—or even the last names—of any of her mother's friends. The neighbors had all changed since Ally had lived with her mother, so there was no one nearby she knew to call. And despite the fact that Ally had continued to try her mother's number again and again in between making arrangements to fly to Chicago as soon as she could, she hadn't ever reached Estelle.

So there she was, on her way to Illinois with no clue what was going on and only her own worst fears to keep her company.

Thank you very much, Jake Fox.

What kind of person made a call like that when something happened to someone's seventy-nine-year-old mother?

No, she and her mother weren't close. And never had been. But Estelle was still her mother. Shouldn't there have been a little compassion? A little finesse? Especially from a medical person?

But Jake Fox had been so impatient. And why? Just because Ally didn't live in the same city, the same state that Estelle lived in? Innumerable people didn't live near family. Ally was sure Estelle wouldn't even *want* her close by, or that close proximity would change the nature of their relationship. Once-a-week phone calls and spending major holidays together, that was the extent of it and would be the extent of it regardless of where she lived.

And who was this guy, anyway? A friend of her mother's from the senior center—that's what he'd said. Was he some sort of boyfriend Estelle hadn't mentioned? Another retiree who had become her companion? And even if they were close, why couldn't he have said what kind of *trouble* her mother was having? Or if Estelle had been hurt. Or where she was…

Ally wasn't a nervous flyer and yet her hands were clenched onto the armrests and her palms were sweaty. Rather than drying her hands on her twill slacks, she decided to make a trip to the restroom to wash them, thinking that getting up, moving around, might help some of her agitation.

It didn't. She was no more relaxed as she ran cool water over her hands, and one glance into the mirror over the sink gave evidence to how tense she was.

She hadn't had time to do more than leave her honey-blond hair loose around a face that had lost the usual bloom of pink that highlighted her cheekbones. Even her slightly full lips looked washed out beneath the thin, straight nose, and her emerald-green eyes were a little bloodshot from lack of sleep.

She dried her hands and smoothed the simple brown T-shirt she wore over the tan slacks before retaking her seat, feeling no better than when she'd left it.

She decided to stop focusing on Dr. Fox. Her mother's health was the only thing that mattered right now.

Please let her be all right...

She took a few deep breaths to combat a fresh rise of fear.

If only her mother was all right, Ally was even willing to have more dealings with Jake Fox. He and his bad, dictatorial disposition were beside the point. Ally just wanted her mother to be okay.

Then she'd deal with Jake Fox.

It was after noon when Ally pulled her rental car up in front of the small suburban home in which she'd grown up.

The two-story, circa-1950s red brick house with its covered front porch looked the same as it always had except that the lawn was dry and nearly dying in spots.

If it had been any other yard in the neighborhood Estelle Rogers would have marched up to the front door, rung the bell, and when the owner had answered, minced no words about how their laziness was lowering her property values. She would have given them a dressing-down that would have shamed them into improved lawn care. So the fact that Estelle's own yard looked so bad in the August heat was an indication that something was amiss.

And Ally needed to go in and see what it was. See her mother.

Ally's stomach—which had been in knots since yesterday's phone call—tied itself into one more. But then, her stomach tied itself into that knot every time she came to visit her mother.

Well, she couldn't sit there and wait it out the way she usually did, so she charged from the car, taking only her purse with her.

"She's not there."

Ally stopped short before even reaching the front porch and turned to find a boy of probably five or six on his bicycle on the sidewalk that ran in front of the house.

"Do you know where she is?" Ally asked, doubting that he did but desperate.

"She got taked 'way in a am-buh-lance today."

Oh God.

Ally's stomach clenched even tighter as awful things went through her mind. Had Estelle been home alone last night when she'd called and called, maybe unable to get to the phone? Had she been lying on the floor all night?

"When was this?" Ally asked the child.

"After breakfast," he answered.

"Do you know where she was taken?" Ally inquired, feeling more frantic by the minute.

"To the hospital," the little boy said as if it should have been obvious.

The neighborhood hospital—she'd start there. And hope she wasn't already too late.

Ally nearly ran down the porch steps and back to her car.

"Thank you," she said to the little boy as she went by him and got behind the wheel again. The hospital was only about a fifteen-minute drive away. Ally made it in ten, parking crookedly in the first spot she could find in the emergency-room lot before she nearly ran to the hospital entrance.

"I'm looking for Estelle Rogers, she may have been brought in by ambulance—"

"Those people are also here about her," the receptionist said, pointing to the waiting room.

Maybe the receptionist didn't want to give her bad news...

Ally turned in the direction the woman indicated. Among the other people in the waiting room, she spotted a group she recognized, if only slightly. Her mother had had routine gallbladder removal four years ago and Ally had come to Chicago then to help Estelle through the surgery and to convalesce afterward. There had been a steady stream of her mother's friends from the Wilkens Senior Center who had visited Estelle during that time, and while Ally didn't remember most of their names, their faces were faintly familiar.

Faces that all looked somber and serious now.

The worst...

The worst has happened...

Ally felt her knees go wobbly. Her head was light. The whole hospital seemed to be spinning.

Without taking a step, she listed to one side and had to grab on to the reception counter's edge.

"Ma'am?"

The receptionist's alarmed voice seemed to be coming from far away.

Then Ally was only vaguely aware of the receptionist jolting to her feet and calling, "Dr. Fox! I need help!"

"So cold! Her hands are like ice, Jacob!"

"It's okay, Bubby. She's coming around."

Ally forced leaden eyelids open. For a moment she was lost. She didn't know where she was, or why she was lying on her back on a hard floor, surrounded by people she barely recognized.

There was a very attractive man hunkered down on one side of her, taking her blood pressure. There was a much, much older woman who had Ally's left hand between both of hers, rubbing vigorously. And there was a woman who looked like a nurse standing at her feet.

It was the blood-pressure-taking and the sight of the nurse that cued memory—she was at the Chicago hospital where her mother had been taken by ambulance.

"My mother…" she said, her own voice sounding fearful and sluggish at once.

"You're who we're interested in right now," the man said, despite the stethoscope in his ears.

Ally looked to the elderly woman rubbing her hand and whispered, "Am I too late? Is she…"

"Oh, no!" the older woman said quickly. "Not Estelle. She had a fall today. And there are some other things wrong, but she's still with us." The hand rubbing became more intense. "Just rest and let our Jacob take care of you."

The man being referred to as "our Jacob" took the stethoscope out of his ears and unfastened the blood pressure cuff from around Ally's arm. As he did, he said, "You thought Estelle had *died?*" He actually looked…embarrassed.

"I didn't know what to think."

"You didn't tell her what's going on?" the older woman demanded of him.

"I told her Estelle was in trouble," he answered, turning even redder.

"Jacob! Look at this poor girl! So worried!"

Now she remembered the woman. Bubby had been the friend that Ally had liked most during Estelle's gallbladder recovery. She was a tiny Jewish lady who had come every day with pastries and casseroles. Rayzel— that was her name.

"She *should* be worried," the man said under his breath.

And that was when Ally knew that *Jacob* was Jake Fox.

She bolted upright, sending her head spinning again. The spinning made her reel, and if Jake Fox's long arm hadn't snaked around her to catch her she would have smacked her head on the wheel of a nearby gurney.

"Hold on! Where do you think you're going?" he said.

"It's you!" Ally accused.

"Lie back down," he commanded, easing her to the floor again before he said, "Yes, we spoke on the phone last night."

His tone wasn't warm, but at least it wasn't as impatient as it had been the previous evening.

Ally realized then that the hospital receptionist and the rest of her mother's friends had gathered around, keeping some distance behind Jake. She hated that she'd made such a spectacle.

"How about a chair?" he said to the nurse. "I think all we have here is a stress-related fainting spell. She doesn't need a bed, but since she wants up, let's let her try to sit. And maybe she can have a little orange juice and a cookie or a cracker…"

With the excitement over, the receptionist returned to her post as the nurse left to do the doctor's bidding. Only Jake Fox and Estelle's friends remained.

Then Jake said to Bubby, "You all can go out and

watch for Nina—you don't want to keep her waiting. I'll deal with this."

"I could stay," Bubby offered. "Nina could take everyone else."

"And miss your card games at the center? No, go on. There's nothing you can do. You know what's happening with Estelle, and her daughter is here now. She's going to be okay. I'll get her back on her feet and she can take over."

After assuring Ally that she would check in with her at dinnertime, Bubby and the contingent of elderly ladies filed out of the emergency room just as the nurse brought a wheelchair into the reception area.

"We can put her in her mother's room," Jake told the nurse. "I'll take her there while you see if you can find the juice and crackers."

"I don't need a wheelchair," Ally protested. Feeling more embarrassed by the minute, she sat up slowly this time so she could stay up.

"I've kept you from having to see an E.R. doctor, but I'm not going to let you on your feet until I'm sure you can stay there," the doctor said flatly.

The nurse put the brake on the chair and left again.

"Let me do the work," the doctor ordered Ally.

His left arm came around her from behind again, he grasped her nearest forearm with his right hand and brought her off the floor and into the chair in one smooth movement as if she weighed nothing.

For no reason she understood, Ally was very aware of the power and strength in that bracing arm and the warmth of his hand on her bare skin. Aware of it all and feeling for the first time as if she wasn't in this alone somehow.

But then she was in the wheelchair and she came to her senses—this was the guy who had read her the riot act and created the stress that had buckled her knees in the first place. Not only was she alone in whatever was happening, but she and Jake were at odds over it, without her even knowing why.

He didn't say anything as he released the brake on the wheelchair and pushed her through the doors that separated the reception area and waiting room from the actual emergency-treatment area.

He took her to one of the small examining rooms that surrounded a central space like satellites. None of the doctors or nurses talking, checking charts or at the computers in the center even looked up, and when they got to Estelle's room it was empty.

"My mother isn't here," Ally said.

"She's probably still in X-ray. I'll check," he said, leaving just as the nurse came in with orange juice and crackers.

Rather than argue, Ally accepted them, taking a few sips of the juice and eating a cracker. Then she tested the sturdiness of her own feet.

She was still a bit shaky, but she made it to the visitor's chair without incident and the nurse wheeled the chair out of the small room.

The nurse met Jake coming back and Ally watched as the two stopped just outside the door to discuss something she couldn't hear. It gave her the opportunity to study the man who had caused her such torment in the last several hours.

He was tall, broad-shouldered, narrow-waisted, and had long legs that were muscular enough to tease the fabric of the khaki slacks he was wearing with a maroon dress shirt and tie.

His hair was a dark espresso brown and he wore it longish and slightly unkempt. He had the facial bone structure of a Greek god—all angles and planes and sharp edges. His nose was hawkish, his lips were lush, and if Ally hadn't disliked him so much from their phone call, she would have been blown away by how good-looking he was.

But appearance aside, he was still the jerk who had verbally skewered her last night and movie-star hand-someness didn't change that.

One thing was for sure, though, he wasn't her mother's boyfriend or companion. He was close to Ally's age—likely in his early thirties—and while it would have surprised her to know her seventy-nine-year-old mother was keeping company with anyone, she knew Estelle wouldn't do anything as audacious as fool around with a younger man.

Which begged the question—why was he hanging out with a group of geriatrics? Maybe he was related to Bubby?

His conversation with the nurse ended just then and he came back into the room.

Propping a hip on one corner of the examining table, he leveled a charcoal-colored gaze on her and Ally tried not to appreciate the beauty of those thickly lashed eyes. Instead, in her most authoritative voice, she said, "Will you please just tell me what's going on with my mother?"

He surprised her with a purely businesslike voice of his own. "I hold groups at the senior center—"

"Groups?"

"I'm a psychiatrist."

"My mother went for therapy?"

"Not exactly. The groups deal with general issues of aging."

"Ah." But if he was a shrink, wasn't that all the more reason that he should have handled things with more tact? Ally thought it was but she didn't say it and he merely went on.

"I also walk every morning with the ladies, so I have pretty consistent contact with Estelle." He paused, sighed slightly and said, "I'm sorry. I didn't want to get into this on the phone and have you think it wasn't that big a problem that you'd have to rush to address. But I started noticing problems with your mother's memory a few months ago. I suggested some supplements, some vitamins that I was hoping might help. But she can be stubborn—and she told me I was crazy, that her memory was as good as ever."

"Only you didn't think that was true?"

"I'm not the only one who's been seeing the changes.

Bubby—who I've known half my life—and the rest of Estelle's friends have also seen them."

So he *wasn't* related to Bubby.

"More than memory changes?" Ally asked rather than get into his personal life.

Jake sighed again. "There's been an all-round slip in her mental state. She gets disoriented, confused. Bubby has been with her twice now when your mother has forgotten the way back from the senior center. Two other friends found her at the mall unable to find her car in the lot—they had to have security drive them up and down the rows until her friends spotted Estelle's car, then one of them drove her home. We've been waiting—and hoping—that you would notice something and step in...but that's never happened."

That last part had a tinge of the previous evening's criticism in it. But since he was allowing her to get her side of the story in, she said, "My mother and I talk on the phone once a week—every Sunday except this last one. But the fact that she doesn't remember what I've told her from one week to the next isn't unusual. She's never been interested enough in what I tell her to make any kind of mental note about it. I've always had to remind her again and again that I'm referring to something I told her. I haven't noticed that being any different."

"Do you ask how she is? Did she tell you about the mall fiasco? You haven't seen or heard anything that seems out of the ordinary?"

Ally thought about it, but she honestly could not

come up with a single instance in which Estelle had seemed like anything but herself.

"No, nothing," she said, even though she knew this man was going to take it as a strike against her. "Every week I ask how she is and she says she's fine—never anything else. When I try to question her about what she's doing, if she's getting out of the house, what might be going on with her friends or at the senior center, she will only say that she's keeping busy, and she gets peeved if I press her for any kind of details, as if I'm prying. Then she cuts me off and that's it for that week's call."

"Maybe she doesn't think you're interested."

So it's still my fault... Ally was getting mad. "Look, Dr. Fox. Things between us just aren't...touchy-feely. On *either* of our parts. She had gallbladder surgery a few years ago and she only told me about that begrudgingly because she said her doctor was going to make her go into some kind of care facility afterward if she didn't have help at home. As soon as I knew, I rearranged my schedule so I could be here and I'd planned to stay longer but after two days she told me she was well enough to take care of herself and that she wanted me to go home."

"Estelle is proud of how independent she is. If she felt as if she was infringing on you or on your time—"

Again it's my fault...

Ally stopped him before he could go any further. "So, were some memory lapses the reason you called me the way you did yesterday?" she asked.

"No," he said simply. "As I said, the ladies and I do a walk every weekday morning. If someone can't make it, they either tell us ahead of time or call one of the group to let us know so no one worries. Yesterday Estelle just didn't show up. I sent the ladies on without me and went to your mother's house. I found her front door wide open, a burner on her stove blazing hot with nothing on it and no Estelle. After searching the place and calling for her, I spotted her from an upstairs window—she was nearly at the other end of the block, wandering down the middle of the street in her nightgown."

That knocked some of the wind out of Ally again.

"Oh."

"Yeah, *oh*. I went after her, got her back home and she was in such a daze she didn't understand why I was upset. She said she'd just gone out to get her newspaper, as if that was all there was to it. I got her some breakfast, but I still didn't want her to be alone. Sylvia— I don't suppose you know her?"

Ally shook her head.

"Well, she's one of your mom's friends, and kindly agreed to stay with her. But by early last night Estelle insisted that she felt fine, that I'd made a big deal out of nothing, and she convinced Sylvia to leave her alone—"

"I must have called the house two dozen times last night and there was never an answer."

"Sylvia had left by the time I talked to you. Who knows why Estelle didn't answer the phone—but that's the point, left to her own devices we don't know what she's doing."

"If all of this was yesterday, how did she end up here today?"

"When she didn't show up for our walk again today the ladies and I all went over there. We can only assume from the way it looked that she'd tripped over a throw rug in the entryway. She'd hit her head, hurt her wrist and she was nearly incoherent."

"And that was when you called the ambulance."

"It was impossible to tell exactly how badly she might have been hurt, so yes, I called the ambulance. She's been examined, and beyond some bumps and bruises, her wrist is the primary concern for the moment—that's why she's in X-ray now. But there's a bigger picture here."

Ally was trying to absorb everything. "I didn't know," she said.

"You don't know what's happening because you're nowhere around," he countered as if he couldn't contain it any longer.

"No, I'm not. I don't live here." The explanation sounded feeble even to her, but it was the best Ally could come up with.

"As people age, as their physical and mental abilities decline, they need help. If they're lucky enough to have family, it's that family that should provide the help."

That was a tidy lecture that once again made Ally feel as if he was passing judgment on her. He was just so convinced that he knew the right way. The only way.

"Well, now that I *am* here, what do you suggest?" she said, challenging his attitude.

In a more reasonable tone, he said, "I've been trying to get your mother to go to her primary-care physician for a physical but she's flat-out refused. I've tried to get her to let me order a brain CT or an MRI, to order blood tests to see if we can tell what's behind the memory lapses, but again, she just won't do it. As her daughter, it's your job to intervene."

"You want me to force my mother to get medical treatment?" Ally said, her own voice taking the opposite turn and becoming louder than it had been.

"Look," he said, as if he felt the need to impress upon her the importance of what he was saying, "Some of what Estelle is showing could be considered indications of Alzheimer's disease. I don't know what your relationship has been in the past, but like I've said already, your mother is in trouble and you're the only family she has."

He had no idea what he was asking of her.

The nurse who had been in before reappeared in the doorway now. "Excuse me, Dr. Fox, but your secretary just called to remind you that you have a patient and the patient's family waiting in your office. There's some volatility…"

Ally looked on as Jake checked his watch. "I completely forgot. Tell Eugenia that I'm on my way."

He glanced at Ally again, his slightly bushy eyebrows coming together in a frown. "How are *you* feeling? Any more light-headedness? Nausea? Dizziness?"

He got points for seeming to care that she'd recovered from her faint and for putting that before whatever volatile situation awaited him.

"I'm fine. I'd just worked myself into such a state of terror on the way over here—that's all it was."

He blushed again. "Look, I'm sorry I scared you."

"It's okay." But Ally was surprised by how small her voice had become.

"Your mother will be back here soon," Jake continued anyway. "They'll probably splint her wrist, give her some pain meds and send her home. You're going to have to take it from there."

Basically what he'd told Bubby.

But Ally had had no idea to what extent he'd meant that when he'd said it earlier. Now that she knew what problems her mother was having and that he expected her to confront Estelle, she felt completely overwhelmed.

Jake was waiting expectantly for some kind of answer, so she nodded her head as if *taking it from there* was exactly what she was agreeing to do—even though she had no idea how she was going to do it.

Apparently he didn't feel reassured. "I mean it. You can't turn a blind eye to this. It has to be dealt with."

"I heard you the first time," she said, managing a little spunk in defense against his once again demanding directive.

He stared at her as if he still wasn't convinced he could leave this in her hands. But after a moment he seemed to concede to the other demands on his time. "I have to go. I'll check with you later, though probably not until tonight."

Ally didn't say anything at all to that, but after another moment, he pushed off the examining table and headed out of the room.

He paused at the door and turned those striking dark gray eyes on her again.

"I'm sorry, Ally," he apologized a third time. "I know this is a lot to handle and none of it is what anyone wants to have to face. But it's in your mom's best interests that you *do* face it," he said, showing the first hint of compassion since they'd met.

"I'll see you later."

Part of Ally would have preferred she never see the man again as long as she lived. Yet another part felt a tiny bit intrigued—and safer—at the idea.

Because as abrasive as the handsome doctor could be, there was also something strong and solid about him that made it seem as if he could handle anything.

And when it came to her mother, Ally wasn't too sure she could.

Chapter Two

It was after eight o'clock Thursday evening. Jake's last session had ended at ten minutes before the hour and he was sitting at his desk in the office that adjoined the hospital trying to make his case notes before he left.

Trying unsuccessfully.

He just couldn't seem to concentrate. Since leaving Ally Rogers at the E.R. he'd done his damnedest to keep his mind on the patients he'd seen. But his thoughts kept wandering back to Ally.

On the few occasions when Estelle had spoken of her daughter, Jake had imagined Ally to be considerably older. After all, he was the age of most of his walking companions' grandchildren, not their children, so he'd never figured that Estelle's *daughter* would be closer to his age.

Young and beautiful...

Yeah, okay, so not only her age had thrown him off.

Ally Rogers was someone any man would have taken a second look at. Which was what he'd been doing from the emergency-room waiting area before he'd even known who she was.

Not too tall—about five-four—she was well proportioned with curves enough for his gaze to linger where it shouldn't have when he'd first seen her from a distance.

She also had gleaming wavy blond hair that was nearly the color of summer sunshine, cascading around a face that could have been made of fine bone china.

But it was her eyes that had stuck with him most. Bright, rich green, the color of rolling Irish hillsides, sparkling even when she was just coming out of her faint...

Not that it mattered, he reminded himself, fighting off the image. It didn't matter how beautiful she was. It didn't matter that she was younger than he'd expected. Neither of those things could excuse neglecting her mother. Or at least what had seemed to *him* like neglect.

It was a personal sore spot with him and he knew it had roots in his own background. Growing up as he had, without a family of his own, shuffled from stranger to stranger in foster care, had bred in him the conviction that families shouldn't be taken for granted. If a person was lucky enough to have one, they damn well should appreciate it and be willing to do whatever it took to maintain it.

Jake threw his pen onto his case file and pushed back into his leather chair with a vengeance.

A tough old bird—that was how he'd always thought of Estelle Rogers. She was a woman who didn't invite closeness, who didn't exude the kind of warmth that Bubby did. But he tended to take people the way they were, to look for the good in them, and he liked Estelle.

Once he'd gotten to know her he'd found that she had a dry sense of humor, an admirable determination and a generous spirit. She was also always ready to lend a hand to anyone at the senior center who needed it, and until recently, she'd played an unbeatable game of cribbage.

But he felt bad for her—lately because of whatever health issues might be looming, and before because she'd seemed as alone as he was, despite the fact that, unlike him, she *did* have family. A daughter.

A daughter who, with the exception of a weekly phone call and a few holiday visits, didn't bother with her mother.

At least, not in the three years that Jake had known Estelle.

Yes, now that he'd met her daughter he was less sure about the relationship between them, but Jake still believed that Estelle was entitled to her daughter's care, difficult relationship or not. And if Ally Rogers had any decency she'd be more conscientious and make the best of however much longer she might have with her mother, because she was lucky to have a mother at all.

On the other hand, clinically, he had to concede that there might be more going on with the Rogerses than he'd thought, and recognizing that battled with those personal feelings.

Some people could be even tougher on their own families than they were on the rest of the world, and maybe Estelle fell into that category. If she did, making the best of the time she and her daughter had left together could be tricky.

The bottom line at this point, though, was that when Estelle's health, well-being and future had to be addressed, her daughter was the only one who could address it. Friends didn't have the same legal authority, if nothing else.

So for Estelle's sake, he hoped Ally could handle the situation the right way.

And maybe for his own sake, too.

Not that he had anything at stake in this other than wanting what was good for Estelle.

It was just that now that he'd seen Ally Rogers, he was hoping she had as much character as she did beauty.

When the doorbell rang at nine o'clock, Ally shot a glance up the stairs of her mother's house, afraid the bell would wake Estelle. She hurried to open the door before whoever was there could ring again.

Jake Fox stood on the step.

Ally considered it a lapse in her own sanity that any part of her was happy to see him. But there was a part that took a little leap of…interest?

Hiding it completely, she said an almost challenging "Hello."

"Hi," he greeted in return.

She asked him in, still camouflaging her secret elation by making the invitation sound begrudging.

But if he noticed, he didn't react to it as he came inside.

What he did react to was the sight of her suitcase, waiting beside the staircase.

"You can't be leaving?" he said. "I checked with the E.R. I know Estelle's wrist is only a sprain and she got a relatively clean bill of health otherwise, but that doesn't mean this is over or under control by any means. The fall is nothing compared to—"

"My mother is upstairs asleep for the night," Ally said to cut him off. "We didn't get out of the emergency room until three this afternoon. I took care of a few things, got us some dinner and since she's finally down for the count I was about to take my suitcase out to my own place."

"Your own place?" he said, sounding calmer but confused.

"There's a small sort-of apartment above the garage. It's where I stay when I'm here."

It was criminal how attractive the man was, even with a baffled expression on his face.

"Come on, I'll show you," she offered rather than

remain where they were and risk that their voices might rouse Estelle.

Ally bent over to pick up her suitcase but Jake beat her to it.

It was an unexpected courtesy.

"Thanks," she said, almost wishing he *hadn't* done anything nice—it conflicted with the ogreish image of him that she was trying to hang on to.

She walked ahead of him down the hallway that ran beside the stairs into the dated liberty-green kitchen. Then she went out the back door and to a stairway that hugged the rear of the house and led to the upper portion of the attached garage.

The stairs creaked as they climbed them to the landing where Ally unlocked a scarred wooden door to let them in.

The apartment was a single room that was more like a big bedroom than an apartment. It was large enough for only a double bed and dresser, a sofa with a television close in front of it, a few kitchen cupboards and some old appliances lining one wall, and a closet and bathroom tucked into the far end.

"This is where you stay when you visit your mother?" Jake asked once they were inside, setting her suitcase on the floor.

"Actually, I haven't lived or stayed in the house with my mother since I was sixteen. I adopted this as my own space then and lived up here through the rest of high school and all through college. After I left home and started coming back to visit, my mother said that she liked her privacy and was sure I'd want mine, so I might as well use it then, too. Which is what I've done."

Ally could see that he found that extremely curious, but since he didn't ask, she didn't say more on the subject.

Instead, he said, "Estelle needs to have tabs kept on her. You can't do that from out here."

"As a matter of fact, I can. One of her friends from the center came by after we got home today and while she and Mother were visiting I went out and bought a state-of-the-art intercom system. It works for every room in the house, so I can monitor where she is at all times. It's also connected to a motion detector that's on the front and the back doors—a light goes on and a beeping sounds whenever either of them opens," she said, pointing at the receiver. "Plus, I don't plan to be up here during the day unless she has a guest or we need a short break from each other."

"Impressive," Jake said with raised eyebrows that made Ally think it surprised him that she'd done anything at all.

She picked up her suitcase from where he'd left it and took it to a trunk at the foot of the bed.

She didn't ask him to sit, wanting to dish out a little payback for his earlier treatment, but also in denial of the fact that she was even slightly glad that he was there.

When she turned back to him she found him perched on the arm of the couch anyway. He looked relaxed and it flashed through Ally's mind that under other circumstances Dr. Jake Fox might have an entirely different effect on her. An effect that would involve things a whole lot better than anger or frustration.

But these *weren't* other circumstances, and to keep even the hint of those better effects at bay, she busied herself by opening windows to air the place out.

"How is Estelle doing?" he asked then.

"Good question," Ally said, hearing the bewilderment in her own voice but glad to talk about her mother to further distract herself when all the windows were open and she had to face him again. "One minute she's herself, and the next...I'm not sure. She did tell me when I brought her home today that I should be a nurse and marry a nice doctor like you—or maybe even you—so I guess we know who she thinks highly of."

He smiled as if she'd caught him off guard with that and he couldn't help himself. And when he smiled, deep grooves bracketed his lips in a way that lent an entirely new level of handsomeness to his features.

Not that she wanted to be aware of that any more than she'd wanted to notice the innate sensuality he exuded just sitting there...

"I'll bet you squashed the idea of me being nice, let alone marriage material," he said wryly.

Okay, so she couldn't help a slight smile, herself, at the fact that he'd read her so correctly.

"You did, didn't you?" he said with a chuckle.

"You're probably married or engaged or living with

someone and she forgot about it," Ally countered rather than admit he was right.

"None of the above. Why? Did she forget that you're married or engaged or living with someone?"

Was he interested, or merely checking on her mother's mental capacities?

He couldn't be interested and as disapproving of her as he'd been.

"No, she didn't forget that about me either—I'm un-attached," Ally confirmed. "What she forgot was that I'm not eighteen and just making my decision about where to go to college and what to major in and do with my life. It was sort of a combination of revisiting a time when she didn't want me to go into interior design and the present-day you thrown in somewhere. It was confusing."

"Yeah, things with Estelle have been that way for a while now."

"But the next minute she can be normal," Ally contributed defensively, because she didn't want him to lose sight of that.

"And the minute after that she could be confused again," he countered. "Did you talk to her about having a physical or letting me order some neurological tests?"

"I tried. More than once. She shot me down every time. Angrily. She says she's fine."

"But you're seeing for yourself that she isn't."

Ally shrugged. "Something is up," she acknowl-edged. "The trouble is, she's the most like herself when she's adamantly refusing to do anything about it."

"That's where you come in."

Ally sighed. "You're barking up the wrong tree if you think that I'm the one who can get my mother to agree to anything. The truth is, I'm the *last* person she listens to."

"Then you'll have to be more take-charge with her than you've ever been before."

"Take-charge? With Estelle Rogers? That would invite a power struggle that would make her dig in her heels worse than she already has. She doesn't do what she doesn't want to do."

Jake's dark gray eyes pinned her in place as he seemed to weigh something.

Then he said, "I'm going to be straight with you, Ally—giving in to Estelle, not doing anything about her health or what's gone on here the last two days, isn't an option. Before you got there today, the E.R. doc wanted to call in Social Services. It can be done for geriatrics the same way it can be done for minors in jeopardy. The fact that Estelle lives alone and that there are indications that it isn't a safe situation for her anymore is enough for them to step in. If they do, they can control what gets done with her and where she ends up living."

Ally could feel the color draining from her face. "Seriously? That can be done with an adult?"

"Anyone considered at risk," he reiterated. "I told the E.R. doc that you were on the way—that kept it from happening today. But if you can't deal with this, I'll have to call a caseworker myself."

"You're threatening me?"

He shook his head. "I'm telling you the way the system works. I can't force a friend to get medical attention, but I am legally obligated to notify authorities if I know of anyone who's unable to care for themselves."

Ally had had just about enough for one jet-lagged, nearly sleepless, enormously stress-filled day. She lost it.

"What do you want me to do, physically force her to have tests done? Apparently you—who she likes and respects and who carries the *authority* of being a doctor—haven't been able to convince her to have the tests you want to do. But you think I can come in here and work some kind of magic on one of the most stubborn people who ever walked the face of the earth? Me, who she still blames for—"

She caught herself. "Who she still thinks of as an irresponsible kid?"

"What does she blame you for?"

Of course. He was a shrink. He wasn't going to let a Freudian slip like that go by.

But Ally wasn't going to bare her soul to him, no matter who he was or what he did for a living.

"It doesn't matter," she said, no longer shouting but sounding no happier with him than she had. "I'm just saying that I'll do whatever I can, but don't expect miracles."

He was watching her closely and she wished she could push a rewind button and go back to the moment before she'd spoken so carelessly. But if he thought silence and scrutiny were going to make her uncomfortable enough to spill more of her guts, he was wrong. Very, very wrong.

Still, when the silence went on longer than she could bear, she sighed and said, "I'll keep working on her and see what I can do. Who knows, since she's changing personalities every hour, maybe she'll wake up tomorrow morning with one that's agreeable. But, Jake, please don't call Social Services until I see if I can fix this."

"It may not be fixable," he cautioned, calmly, quietly, and in a way that told her he was going to drop his quest for an explanation. "If Estelle has Alzheimer's—"

"Can we just stick to what I can deal with this weekend while I'm here?"

"This *weekend?* This weekend is only the beginning."

And he was on the attack again—Ally heard that familiar impatience in his voice.

"If your mother has Alzheimer's," he continued, "there won't be an easy solution. And one way or another—"

"I know!" she said to stop him from saying more that she just couldn't hear tonight. "I know, I know, I know!"

Exhausted, Ally sank onto the corner of her bed.

To his credit, he got the message that she simply could not handle the big picture right then.

He switched gears, his tone calmer, more consoling. "Why don't I see if Bubby can come over tomorrow? She can be persuasive—and as stubborn as they come if she needs to be. Maybe if the two of you gang up on your mother, she'll listen."

"An intervention of two?" Ally said facetiously.

"Pretty much. I'd make it an intervention of three but I'm the keynote speaker at a conference tomorrow that I can't miss. But if you and Bubby together can't get through to your mother tomorrow, I promise I'll add whatever influence I have to convince her to have those tests done."

Ally had been staring at the floor but she glanced at him then, finding a kind smile on his face.

He got up and came to stand in front of her, reaching a big hand to her arm and squeezing it comfortingly. "I know this is rough."

Did he also know how warm his hand was? How strong? How good it felt and that something elemental in her sparked?

"Let's just take it a day at a time for now," he added, his deep voice drawing her from her thoughts. "Tomorrow we'll bring in reinforcements with Bubby, and then we'll go from there."

Ally nodded.

"Get some rest," he advised.

Ally nodded again, shocked by how sorry she was when he let go of her arm.

She got to her feet. "I'll walk you out and peek in on my mother to make sure she's still asleep."

Jake led the way for the trip back through the house, opening the front door when he reached it.

But he didn't immediately go out. Instead, he turned to look at her. "I'll check in again tomorrow night."

Ally nodded, gazing up into those smoldering eyes and suffering another wave of that strange mix of emotions that volleyed back and forth between hating this guy and being confused by the feelings he stirred in her.

"I'll be here," she answered.

"That's important," he said before he reached for her arm again and did another of those reassuring squeezes.

Only this time he rubbed his thumb against her arm, too, and somehow that made it seem less comforting and more…intimate.

But then he said good-night and left, and Ally wasn't sure if she had only imagined that.

Chapter Three

"I'll have to take this."

David Hanson excused himself from the dinner table to take a phone call. When he did, Nina Hanson's children—Zach and Izzy—asked if they could be excused as well. That left only Jake, Bubby and Nina—who was Bubby's granddaughter and Jake's friend since they'd met as teenagers—sitting in the Hansons' dining room.

It was Friday evening. Jake had a standing invitation to the traditional Shabbat celebration that Nina held each week. As part of the religious observance, Nina, Bubby and the kids lit candles, said kiddush, and afterward they all enjoyed a meal together. And even though Jake wasn't Jewish, he liked to be there whenever he

VICTORIA PADE 43

could because it was a warm family time that gave him a sense of belonging that was almost as good as having a family of his own.

"Poor David," Nina said with a loving look in the direction her husband had just gone to take his phone call. "He's probably going to have to go to Kyoto next week while Tom Holloway goes to San Francisco. There's trouble with both the Taka hotels."

Jake knew that Nina's husband's family business— Hanson Media—had merged with a Japanese-owned company called Taka Corporation a few years ago and that as a result, their business interests had expanded. They were now in the process of developing a chain of upscale hotels, with the first two in San Francisco and Japan.

"What's going on?" Jake asked.

"There are accounting irregularities in Kyoto," Nina said. "And the promises the interior designer made that he would get back on schedule by this month have fallen through. That puts the soft opening of the Taka San Francisco in jeopardy."

"Does Drake Thatcher have anything to do with it all?" Jake asked. Nina had told him just last month that the tycoon had planted a woman named Shelly Winston within David's organization to spy and sabotage things from inside. It hadn't been successful because Shelly Winston and Tom Holloway—the new head of corporate finance of the hotel division—had fallen in love and ended up together, but it seemed to follow that any other unexpected occurrences might track back to Thatcher, too.

"They don't know. Anything is possible at this point," Nina answered. "All I know is that things are a mess."

"Speaking of messes," Bubby interjected. "I visited with Estelle and Ally this afternoon, Jacob."

Nina didn't seem to mind her grandmother's abrupt change of subject, because she began to stack all the dirty dishes she could reach from where she was sitting. And since Jake had been anxious to ask Bubby what had come of her trip to Estelle's house today, he welcomed finally being able to get into it.

"I didn't want to bring the subject up with David and the kids around—I knew it wasn't anything they'd be interested in—but I was going to ask you about it as soon as I had the chance. How was Estelle today?"

"The same—sometimes the old Estelle, some-times…" Bubby raised both palms toward the ceiling, shrugging her shoulders at the same time to convey her own lack of understanding of what was happening with her friend. "She's a handful, that Estelle," Bubby con-cluded. "She went to the bathroom, never came back. We found her packing her bag. She said her husband called and wanted her to go on a business trip with him—the man's been dead forever!"

"And what did her daughter think of that?" Jake saw Nina's eyebrows rise and he knew his victorious tone of voice had been the cause, so he explained himself. "I had a hard time convincing the daughter that there's a problem."

"Poor Ally, she can tell her mother's not right in the

head now," Bubby said sympathetically. "This is a lot for that girl to take in, Jacob. We've all been seeing Estelle slip, but her daughter—"

"Would have seen it, too, if she'd had more to do with her."

"Oy, such a big deal with this one!" Bubby said to her granddaughter.

Nina laughed. "You know how he is—he can't believe anybody who has a family can take it for granted. But he does seem awfully invested in this particular family, doesn't he?" she responded to Bubby as if Jake wasn't there. "Do you think it has anything to do with how pretty you said Estelle's daughter is?"

"Pretty?" Bubby exclaimed. "Pretty doesn't do her justice. And me? I saw Jacob at the hospital—before he knew who Ally was, when she just came in the door and was at the reception counter? His eyes were glued to her. He didn't even hear Ruth Cohen ask him if he wanted a cup of coffee out of the machine. It was like in the movies when everything else fades away and he only knew there was her."

Jake shook his head at the absurdity of that. Yes, Ally Rogers had caught his attention, but it didn't mean anything. "The key word in all of that is *before*—before I knew she was the daughter who neglected Estelle."

"What neglect? When Estelle needed Ally for the gallbladder, Ally came. Estelle hasn't needed her for anything else until now, and where is she now? Here again, that's where. So what neglect? Those foster homes, those group places you had to grow up in, Jacob, they made you daydream of what real families are. But it's not so realistic. Families—there's some good, there's some not so good—families are families. What they're not is fairy tales."

"If you're even a little pale one day, Bubby, isn't Nina going to notice it? And why? Because she sees you. She knows you. She knows what's going on with you. Would I have to call her and order her to go to your apartment? Would I have to tell her to help you? No, I wouldn't."

"Not everyone is like my Nina. But that doesn't mean Ally is a bad girl. And Estelle is a hard nut to crack—you know that. How many weeks have you been trying to get her to have a checkup? Where has it gotten you? You called Ally, she came—where's the crime?"

"The crime is if she turns around and goes back to California without taking care of her mother."

Again Bubby looked at Nina. "He wants this one to be so perfect."

"He does seem to want her to live up to something, doesn't he?"

"He wants her to *be* as good as she looks."

"I just want her to do what she needs to do. For Estelle," Jake insisted.

"Well, she did—how does that make you think of her?" Bubby challenged.

"What did she do?"

"Between the both of us we got Estelle to say she would have your tests." The victory was all Bubby's now.

"You got Estelle to agree?"

"We did. She won't see her own physician, though. She likes you—that's what Ally used to make her say she would."

"I'll get right on it, then," Jake said.

"And say some sorries to that girl, Jacob," Bubby ordered. "You're too hard on her."

"I have not been *too* hard on her," he defended himself. "I've been as hard as I needed to be to open her eyes. Why? Did she complain to you?"

"No, but I can tell from her attitude. Enough, already! She's scared enough. This is bad, don't make it worse."

Bubby stood, picked up the pile of dirty dishes that Nina had stacked and headed for the kitchen.

But while the elderly woman may have seen the subject of Ally Rogers as closed, Jake had one more question.

"Do you know what Estelle blames Ally for?"

Bubby stopped short to look at him. "Blame? What's to blame?"

"I don't know. Last night Ally said Estelle blames her for something, but she wouldn't say what."

"I don't know about that. I just know this—tonight is the night to celebrate the end of the week, to reflect, and then to usher in the start of a new week. A new week brings a new chance to do right. Start the new week by being nicer to that girl, Jacob. You'll get further." Then Bubby smiled slyly at him. "And who knows? Maybe you could end up with that family of your own after all."

Bubby disappeared into the kitchen and Jake turned

his focus to his old friend, thinking Nina would be on his side and understand that there was nothing personal going on between himself and Ally Rogers.

But Nina seemed to agree with her grandmother, because she was barely hiding a knowing smile of her own.

The knock on Ally's apartment door at nine on Friday night startled her.

Her initial, panicked thought was that her mother had gotten out of the house without the alarm going off.

But then it occurred to her that if Estelle got out of the house, the last place she was likely to come was here.

She peeked out the curtain over the window that allowed her a view of the outside landing. And then the late visit made sense—Jake Fox again. He had said he would check in with her today.

Better late than never. Not that she cared.

"I wondered who would know to come back here," she said in greeting when she opened the door.

"The house was all dark so I figured Estelle had gone to bed early again. I took the chance that you'd still be up and came around," he explained amiably.

In fact, nothing about Jake's demeanor said he was on the offensive tonight. He actually seemed relaxed— more even than when he'd perched on the arm of her sofa the night before.

Ally couldn't help being suspicious of it, though. Even as she found herself unwillingly attracted to it.

"Come in," she invited.

"Thanks."

She couldn't help sneaking a glance at him over her shoulder as she closed the door behind him. He looked great. Whatever had occupied him earlier in the evening must have begun immediately after work because he was dressed much the way he had been on Thursday— casual cocoa-colored twill slacks and a pale yellow dress shirt with the sleeves rolled up. The only thing missing was a tie. Plus, there was the slight shadow of beard darkening his face, but it only added an appealingly masculine scruffiness that Ally didn't want to like as much as she did.

"I talked to Bubby," he announced as soon as Ally turned to face him.

"She brought lunch over and stayed most of the afternoon—it was really nice of her," Ally informed him.

"And she said you two finally got your mother to agree to let me order tests."

"It took some work but, yes, we did. Mother won't have a full physical, but she said she'd let you do what you want. I've reminded her about a million times since then that that was what she'd said she would do so she wouldn't forget."

"How did that go?"

"She got annoyed and irritated with me, but as of when she went to bed, she was still saying she'd go through with it."

"Great! I made some calls, pulled some strings, and even though tomorrow is Saturday, I've arranged for her to have a brain scan and blood work at the hospital. The labs will tell us if anything systemic is going on, the brain scan will let us know if she's suffered a stroke—"

"A stroke? That's the first you've said anything about that." Why was it that every time she talked to this guy, things seemed to get worse?

He sighed. "You're right. I'm getting ahead of myself. A stroke is another possibility, yes," he said. "She could have had one in the part of her brain that affects memory, and we could be seeing the damage from that. Or there could be a small aneurysm that's bleeding into that portion of her brain—"

Worse and worse...

"That's why we need the scan, to rule out these other things. If there's no evidence of a stroke or an aneurysm, and nothing systemic to explain what's going on with her, then we move to the second stage and I'll do cognitive tests for Alzheimer's."

Just when Ally thought she might be getting a grip on what she could be dealing with, he added to the list of scary possibilities and made her feel overwhelmed again.

There was a tiny two-chair kitchen set against the wall near the door. Ally pulled out one of the chairs and sat down, not caring any longer if it was rude to sit when she hadn't asked him to.

Jake didn't wait to be invited to join her. He just did, pulling the other chair from the opposite side of the drop-leaf table to the front of it so he was closer to her when he sat down. Close enough for her to catch a whiff of an outdoorsy cologne.

"I know, I'm the bearer of bad news," he said as if he'd read her mind. "It's not a role I like."

Had that contributed to his harshness of before?

She expected him to talk more about the tests and what they could reveal and how bad it could all be, but he didn't. Instead, he said, "You and I haven't had a wonderful start, and I think I owe you an apology."

Ally stared at him, trying to figure out if she'd missed something.

"Bubby says I've been too hard on you," he added.

"I didn't say anything like that to her," Ally defended herself.

"I know. She said she could just tell. But she's right, I *have* been a little rough on you. Partly because I hate what's happening with Estelle, hate not being able to put my head in the sand about it, and partly because I sometimes have unreasonably high expectations of family members—that part comes from my own history—"

"A history of your own family meeting or not meeting your expectations?"

He hesitated for a moment. "I don't have any family."

"Oh."

But he didn't give her the chance to probe into it any further. "Anyway, when I'm dealing with my patients and their relatives, I'm good at keeping my personal feelings under wraps. But you got me in personal mode and… Well, like I said, I know I was rough on you. But the important thing is that you *are* here, doing what you can for Estelle now that you know that something is wrong. So how about if we put everything else behind us and start fresh?"

Ally still wasn't sure whether or not to drop her guard with this man. But she'd appreciated Bubby's help with her mother today and if Bubby had gone to bat for her with Jake Fox, it seemed only fair to accept the olive branch he was offering as a result.

"You have been sort of awful to me," Ally said, unwilling to give him a completely free pass.

He smiled sheepishly—and very engagingly. "But was it so bad that it's unforgivable?"

Ally pretended to consider that. But then she conceded. "I suppose *unforgivable* is a bit of a stretch."

"So I'm forgiven?"

His smoky voice was a blend of humor and mischievous contrition. There was a glimmer in his gray eyes, and one eyebrow arched—the man *could* be charming when he wanted to...

And it took Ally a moment to stop basking in it all.

"You're only forgiven if I've seen the last of that mean guy," she warned, wishing her tone hadn't come out slightly on the coy side.

"I'm on probation then?"

"Actually, I guess you are," she said. "Because if the mean guy comes out to bite off my head again I'd just as soon not see any more of you." Handsome, hunky and charming or not.

But her ultimatum only seemed to amuse him. "Okay, I guess I had that coming. Let's just work together for Estelle's benefit and see if I can't prove myself while we do."

"How will we work together?"

"For starters, tomorrow I'll pick up the two of you, take you both to the hospital and stick with you through the tests. There's only so much friends can do to get the ball rolling with someone like Estelle, but once it *is* rolling, we can be there for all the help and support you need."

"Are we going to be friends?" Ally challenged.

"At least," he countered with some devilishness to his expression.

He couldn't be flirting with her, could he?

That just didn't seem likely.

And yet, she had the sense that he was.

She was still trying to figure it out when he abruptly got to his feet. "I should go. I haven't been home since six this morning," he announced.

Feeling more steady, Ally stood again, too.

"What time tomorrow?" she asked, following him to the door.

"I'll be here at about one. Be prepared for some waiting, though—I've made these arrangements with an emergency-room doctor who's a friend of mine. We'll go in there, he'll order labs and the CT, but if the E.R. is busy—"

"Everyone else will go ahead of us because we'll be there on the sly," Ally guessed.

"Right. But we'll still get the tests done and get the results right away—that's the advantage of the E.R."

The results...

The color felt as if it drained from her face and it must have because he smiled at her again, compassionately this time.

"It's better to know what you're dealing with, Ally. And by tomorrow night we'll have more to go on," he said.

Ally nodded even though she wasn't entirely sure if he was right. Sometimes ignorance *was* bliss.

He raised his hand to press the backs of his fingers to her cheek as if to test for temperature. "Are you gonna faint on me again?" he asked with a hint of amusement in his deep voice.

"No, I'm fine," she said, unusually aware of the feel of his skin against hers.

"We'll handle whatever we need to, you know?" he assured.

He was pretty free with those *we's*. And yet, somehow, it was reassuring.

He took his hand away from her cheek, but his eyes were still on hers, and if this had been any other situation she might have thought he was going to kiss her.

But this situation was a long, long way from a kissing-good-night situation, and she wasn't even sure why that had crossed her mind.

"Tomorrow at one," she repeated when neither of them had said anything for what seemed like a while and they were still standing at the door staring into each other's eyes.

"Call me if Estelle gets up in the morning and forgets

she agreed to do this. I'll come earlier and we'll go to work on her like you and Bubby did today so we can still get her there during my friend's shift."

"Keep your fingers crossed that she remembers," Ally advised.

He raised that same big hand that had been on her face a moment before and showed her crossed fingers. "You, too."

She did the same and he touched the tip of his to the tip of hers as if they were toasting something. And a little jolt of electricity went from him into her, sending a tingling up her arm.

He opened the door then and stepped out onto the landing. "Get some sleep," he suggested.

Ally raised her chin as if she intended to, when the truth was, worry was keeping her from getting more than minimal rest and she still felt jet-lagged.

"See you tomorrow," she said.

He nodded and headed down the stairs with Ally watching him go, watching him until he disappeared around the corner of the house to get to the front.

Then she closed the door and turned from it, catching the faintly lingering scent of his cologne.

And even though she didn't understand why, she couldn't resist breathing it in deeply and picturing Jake all over again.

Jake standing at the door, facing her, towering above her in all his broad-shouldered, masculine majesty.

Jake looking into her eyes.

Jake with his hand against her cheek.

Jake in a position from which he could easily have kissed her...

Ally yanked herself back to reality.

Kissing Jake Fox?

She shook her head and went back to the kitchen. "Maybe I should have my head examined, too."

Chapter Four

"You know, when you first called me and said you were a friend of my mother's, I thought you must be in her age bracket," Ally said to Jake as they sat at a table in the hospital cafeteria late Saturday afternoon.

"That makes sense," Jake allowed.

It had been a relatively busy day in the emergency room, which meant that despite the fact that they'd arrived at one-thirty, it was nearly four before Estelle was taken for her CT scan. Jake and Ally had gone to the cafeteria for coffee.

Jake took a sip and then said, "I thought you'd be older, too. Most of Estelle's friends' kids are in their fifties."

Estelle had monopolized Jake since he'd picked them

up, so this was actually Ally's first chance to talk to him. Her mother had basically left her out of the conversation as Estelle and Jake had discussed people and events Ally had no knowledge of, and although she didn't want to admit it, she'd felt a little jealous. Jealous of how easy it was for Jake to relate to her mother when she always found it to be a struggle, and jealous of Jake's attention to Estelle, too.

That jealousy was not made easier by the fact that he looked terrific dressed more casually in khaki slacks and a yellow polo shirt. It wasn't made easier by the fact that he smelled good, or that the charm of the previous evening had been in play today, too.

He looked good, he smelled good, he was charming, nice, personable—it was all working together to effectively dim the memory of his bad start with her. And now that she had him alone, she was more interested in him than in explaining why the daughter of a seventy-nine-year-old was only thirty-one.

So she didn't offer an explanation and instead said, "How did it come about that you hang out with a group of…" She was a little afraid that she might refer to her mother and her mother's friends in a way that would set him off. She settled on, "women of advanced years?"

"It isn't only women. I hang out with some advanced-years men, too," he said, making fun of her cautious choice of words. "It's just that the advanced-years women outnumber the men, so there are fewer men making up my posse."

Ally had to smile at that. "Your *posse?*" she repeated, happily surprised to discover that he had a sense of humor on top of the other appealing things she was coming to see him capable of.

"That's right, we're the Silver Dogs," he said, keeping up the patter. "Walkin' our three miles a day, blowin' those sweet retirement checks on cinnamon buns, hittin' the streets to stir up trouble, maybe score some antacids and bunion pads on the black market."

"Okay, okay," Ally stopped him, laughing. "I get it—you're the Wild Bunch."

"Age isn't a big deal to me," he said then, without the humor. "We're all just friends."

"But that still doesn't tell me how you got involved with them."

"Through Bubby. I've been friends with her grand-daughter Nina Hanson since we were both teenagers. That's how I met Bubby, so I've known—and loved—Bubby for half my life. She hooked me up."

Another note of levity. Ally didn't know if he was doing it purposely to ease the tension of being at the hospital again, of setting the wheels in motion to find out what was wrong with her mother, but it was helping even if that wasn't what he had in mind.

"Why did Bubby hook you up with them?" she asked.

"I have a lot of geriatric patients in my private practice. I'm also on staff here, so I see a lot of seniors when they come into the hospital. Bubby knows that. She talked me into doing a few counseling groups at the

Wilkens Center—grief and loss, adjusting to the changes of aging, things like that. That's where I met your mom."

"You said that that first time we met, but you said Mother hadn't exactly gone to you for therapy," Ally reminded him.

"Some of the groups are serious, by-the-book therapy, and, no, Estelle hasn't come to any of those. Some are more social, more chitchat—we've hashed through getting one group converted to online banking so their social-security checks don't come in the mail and get stolen out of their mailboxes. But the social groups have therapeutic value, too—isolation can breed depression."

"And the social groups are what Mother has joined," Ally guessed. "Until you said it, I didn't know you were part of the weekday walking—I thought it was just Mother and her friends. But if you're in on that, does that mean it's one of your sort-of-socializing counseling groups?"

"No, the walking group really is just a bunch of friends and—like I said—I happen to be one of them. It *did* get its start at the center, in the counseling groups, though. I encourage exercise in all of the groups, but that wasn't getting the job done—it needed some organizing, some implementing. Pretty much everybody who uses the senior center lives near it and so do I. I suggested we meet mornings in the park that's central to us all, and it worked—several of the seniors from the center started showing up—including Bubby and Estelle.

"We've been at it for four years now. Three miles a day, Monday through Friday, through all but the worst weather. We walk, we talk, we've all gotten to know each other pretty well."

He paused to drink more coffee, but his eyes never left her. Then he added, "Which is why I'm wondering now why I don't know more about you."

"Probably because I'm not my mother's favorite thing to talk about," Ally muttered. Then, as if she hadn't, she said, "What do you want to know?"

"Why you make comments like that, for one."

"What *else* do you want to know?"

He smiled at her blatant diversion. "Okay, how about something easy? Like, what do you do for a living—I can't remember Estelle ever saying."

"I'm an interior designer."

"Do you work for yourself?"

"Well, yes, I'm the Ally Rogers in Ally Rogers Designs. But I work for whoever hires me."

"And you're in L.A., so does that make you the decorator to the stars?"

He said that as if it were a headline and Ally laughed again. "I do have a celebrity-heavy client list."

"You must be good at what you do," he said as if he was impressed.

"I hope so."

"And you could tell me what color tile is on the bathroom walls of the biggest names in Hollywood?"

Ally laughed once more at his mock-starstruck act.

"I could, but then I'd be breaching confidentiality," she said as if she were the medical professional.

"I'll bet you could whip my place into shape, couldn't you?"

That wasn't an invitation and yet the idea of seeing his place gave Ally a little tingle of excitement.

She told herself that was crazy and said, "Does your place need whipping into shape?"

"Probably. I go for comfort not style. I can't believe it wouldn't give the decorator to the stars nightmares."

"What about you?" Ally countered, making it his turn. "How did you decide to become a psychiatrist?"

He'd finished his coffee and pushed his cup away.

"You're not going to tell me how you decided to become a psychiatrist?" she persisted.

He shrugged a shoulder and her gaze fell there and to the big bicep below it that stretched the polo shirt's short sleeve to the maximum—apparently he did more in the way of working out than merely walking.

"I grew up around a lot of people who had mental and emotional problems," he finally said.

"You did? And you said last night that you don't have any family—could this be another piece of the Jake Fox puzzle?"

He smiled a secretive sort of smile that said he was no more willing to be open with her than she had been with him. "Anyway," he went on, "I saw how much suffering and turmoil there could be for psych patients and even for the rest of us who might have some things to deal with—"

There was emphasis on that and a pointed poke of his chin at her to let her know he was referring to her and Estelle.

But he didn't push it, picking up where he'd left off to finish. "I just wanted to help, and in the process of getting some therapy of my own it struck me that being a psychiatrist was a good route to that."

"You were in therapy?"

"I was," he admitted unashamedly, giving her another puzzle piece.

"So you didn't just grow up around people with emotional and mental-health issues—you had some yourself?" Ally ventured, extending it as a challenge because she was wondering about him more and more with every clue he gave and she was hoping the question might provoke some candor.

But Jake only smiled again to let her know he wasn't taking the bait. "Everybody has issues."

"I don't know," she said. "Maybe you're one of those brilliant but completely loony guys and you aren't a doctor at all, you're just posing as one and you've fooled this whole hospital."

"Want to see my credentials?" he asked in a wicked tone of voice, making her laugh yet again before he said, "The proof that I'm a bona fide M.D. is that I can drink hospital coffee."

"That's true," she played along, grimacing at her own cup. "A person would have to have some serious desensitizing for that."

He checked his watch then and Ally realized that if his intention had been to get her mind off the pending problems with her mother he'd done a good job. Until that moment she had been allowed a little break from the worry.

But she knew what he was going to say now...

"Well, Alice..."

Okay, so she hadn't known he was going to use the name he'd heard her mother call her. He hadn't used it the rest of the time. But he did seem to enjoy teasing her with it at that moment.

Ally grimaced. "Not Alice. *Never* Alice."

"That's what your mother calls you," he said like an ornery kid.

"And *only* my mother, who I can't get to stop calling me that, no matter how hard I try."

"Alice is a nice name," he said.

"Not when my mother says it, so I've never liked it," she answered, again somewhat under her breath.

"See—issues," he pointed out.

Ally rolled her eyes at him, but when she didn't remark he finished what he'd been about to say.

"Well, Ally-*not*-Alice, we should get back. Estelle will just about be done in radiology."

Ally took a deep breath to bolster herself for the return to the task and tension of the day and stood.

Jake got to his feet, too.

There was a restroom at the entrance to the cafeteria and when they reached it Ally paused. "I'm going to make a quick pit stop."

"Think you can find your way to the E.R.? I'd hate to have no one be there if Estelle gets back."

"I'll only be a minute, but I'm sure I can follow the signs if you want to go ahead."

"I'll see you there then," he said.

Without warning he reached out and grasped her arm much as he had that first night when he'd left her mother's house, giving it a gentle but firm squeeze and a brush of his thumb.

The gesture caught her by surprise as much today as it had before. Only today, in public, it seemed to carry with it not only a sense of comfort, but an even greater air of intimacy and a feeling of connection between them.

"See you back there," she echoed quietly as she wondered what there was about this man that made the slightest thing throw her out of whack.

That reaching out of his was just a reflex, she told herself. It was just something he did. She didn't believe it meant anything to him. So it shouldn't—couldn't—mean anything to her.

Yet as she went into the restroom, she could still feel his hand where it had made contact with the bare skin of her upper arm.

And it *did* mean something to her.

It meant that it was way too easy for him to get to her.

"Ally Rogers? That *is* you, isn't it? I thought it was when I saw you in the cafeteria!"

Ally was hurrying to the sink in the hospital restroom to wash her hands so she could follow Jake back to the E.R. to wait for her mother to be returned from her CT scan. She stopped short and studied the woman in the nurse's uniform who had just come in. It took a moment before she realized who the woman was.

"Gretchen Fuller?"

"In the flesh—still fat and sassy!" the nurse confirmed.

"You were never fat!" Just a nice kind of fluffy that made her good to hug—which Ally did.

They'd gone to high school together but lost touch second year of college when Gretchen had gotten married and moved to Iowa.

At the end of the hug, Ally said, "You moved back?"

"About four years ago. Teddy and I were both homesick and now that we have three kids, we wanted to cash in on some free babysitting from the families."

"*Three* kids?"

"All boys—I live in testosterone town! We're thinking about a fourth, to try one more time for a girl before it's too late, but we haven't decided for sure. What about you? Married? Kids?"

Ally shook her head. "Neither."

"No wonder you look so good!" Gretchen exclaimed, rearing back to give Ally the once-over. "You put me to shame, you're so beautiful!"

"Hardly," Ally demurred, embarrassed.

"You could be right out of a fashion magazine with that adorable outfit. And those sandals are gorgeous! I'll bet they cost what I spend at the grocery store to feed three kids for a month!"

Ally had no idea how much groceries for three kids for a month cost, but she thought Gretchen could be right since the shoes were Italian and the price had made Ally's jaw drop. But she'd loved them, bought them, and worn them today *because* they were so fabulous and her entire outfit had been chosen carefully, knowing it shouldn't matter what she wore to a hospital to find out if there was something wrong with her mother, and yet it did—because she would be spending the afternoon with Jake Fox.

Uncomfortable with her old friend's scrutiny, though, she changed the subject. "When did you become a nurse?"

"Right after we left Chicago. We were in Iowa City, Teddy was doing his residency in pathology, the kids hadn't started to come yet, I was bored and there was a nursing program, so I just thought why not?"

"You must like it if you're still doing it with three kids at home."

"What I like is getting out of the house for a few shifts a week so I can talk to adults and someone else can change diapers and holler at my kids."

Ally laughed, thinking that Gretchen was right about herself—she was still sassy.

"I don't have to ask what you're doing," Gretchen said then. "I've seen your name in the home-and-garden magazines I'm addicted to, so I looked you up on the Internet—you're the Ally Rogers who decorates all those fancy movie stars' houses!"

"It's a dirty job but someone has to do it," Ally joked.

"Only here you are now—and with our Jake Fox! I saw the two of you—"

There was insinuation in that and Ally shook her head quickly to disabuse her old classmate of whatever it was Gretchen was thinking.

"I'm here with my mother. She's been having some problems and she's undergoing tests today."

"Oh, I'm sorry to hear that. I hope she'll be all right."

"Thanks. Me, too."

"Then you haven't moved back?"

"No! I'm only here temporarily, to deal with what's going on with Mother and then I'll go home to L.A."

"Really?"

Why the doubt?

"Really," Ally confirmed.

"Because I *saw* you and Jake…"

"Having coffee?" Ally asked, confused by the insinuation that had returned to her friend's voice.

"The two of you seemed really into each other."

"*Into* each other? We were only talking. He's a friend of my mother's, he arranged for the tests she's having today and is just keeping us company."

"Huh. Well, you'd be lucky to snag him—maybe you should think about it."

Ally laughed. "I don't think I want to *snag* anyone."

"But Jake Fox," Gretchen said with adoration. "Just about everyone around here has a crush on him. Even me, although I'd never let Teddy know," she whispered.

Then in a normal voice again she said, "And not only is he the best eye candy I've ever seen in person, he's as nice as they come. When Teddy's grandmother died last year his grandfather went downhill fast from the grief. We thought we were going to lose him, too, just from a broken heart. But we got him in to see Jake and what a sweetheart he was! He just turned Teddy's grandfather around. We were so grateful to him."

"My mother and her friends are fond of him, too."

"And you're not?" Gretchen said facetiously, as if Ally was trying to put one over on her. "Because you never took your eyes off him in the cafeteria."

"We were just talking," Ally repeated.

"And smiling and laughing—I was two tables away trying to get your attention to see if it really was you and you didn't know anyone else was even in the cafeteria."

Okay, so maybe she *had* been devouring the sight of the man. In her defense, she'd been trying to figure out why it seemed as if the more she looked at that handsome face of his, the more she found to like about it. But there was no way she was going to admit that.

Gretchen whispered again as if they weren't the only ones in the restroom, "Is it a secret?"

"No, it isn't a secret. There's honestly nothing between us. I barely know him."

Though for some reason, the truth in that made her feel a tiny bit melancholy.

"Well, I'm telling you, you should think about it,"

Gretchen urged. "You couldn't do better than Jake Fox. And you'd be good for him, too. The last girlfriend he brought around was wrong for him. We could all see it—she wasn't his type."

Ally knew she should cut this off to get back to the emergency room. But even so she heard herself say, "How was she not his type?"

"She was all about her career, she'd barely say hello and then go outside to use her cell phone as if none of us were worth wasting her precious time. And that's *sooo* not Jake. No matter how busy he is, he'll always ask how you are and listen when you tell him. And the way he is with his older patients? He'll sit with them forever while they tell their stories—and some of them can talk your ear off!"

"But that *is* what a psychiatrist does, isn't it? Listen?" Ally pointed out.

"Oh, this is above and beyond the call of duty. But that last girlfriend would get so put out if she had to wait for him. I saw her pacing outside a patient's room one night, huffing and puffing and tapping her foot because he was in there just sitting on the edge of the bed while a ninety-year-old talked about her first dance. I knew then that it would never work."

"And apparently it didn't?" Why was she digging for dirt on Jake Fox's love life? Especially when she should be getting back to her mother?

"They broke up not long after that," Gretchen said. "I don't know why or who broke off with who or anything, but if you want my opinion, he dodged a bullet. As far as I know, he hasn't had much action since then so he should be ripe for the picking. And like I said, there's no shortage of women around here who wouldn't give anything to sink their claws into him. If you have the inside track, you should go for it." Gretchen nudged Ally with an elbow. "Besides, you better get busy to catch up with me."

Ally merely smiled and nodded, but Gretchen didn't seem to notice her lack of comment because the nurse glanced at her watch and said, "I have to go back to the floor. Any chance we could get together while you're in town? I'd love it if you could come by the house, meet the kids…"

"I think I'll have to take a rain check, Gretch. Mother can't be left alone right now and—"

"I understand. Maybe next trip." Then Gretchen winked. "And if you spend your time now with Jake, maybe he'll get you to move back for good and then we can pick up where we left off all those years ago!"

Again Ally merely nodded and smiled, thinking that nothing and no one would ever get her back to Chicago for good.

Gretchen gave her another hug and then left Ally to finally wash her hands.

As she did, she couldn't help thinking about what her old friend had said, particularly about the woman Jake had been involved with. It obviously hadn't occurred to Gretchen that some of her description of that other

woman—the woman who had been wrong for him—
applied to Ally.

No, she wasn't someone who huffed or puffed or
tapped her feet to show her displeasure. But she was definitely all about her career. So far, for her, that's what
came first and she couldn't picture it being demoted.

Which meant that *she* was wrong for Jake, too.

Not that she'd thought she was right for him. Or
thought about it at all. Or wanted to be right for him. Of
course she was wrong for Jake Fox. So what?

And yet something about the suddenly blatant
knowledge of that didn't sit well with her.

But she *did* love her work. And her busy, hectic,
career-first life in Los Angeles. And she *wouldn't*
change any part of it.

Although she had to admit that every now and then,
when she was facing a long weekend or a holiday or
even time between projects, she sometimes didn't know
what to do with herself. She sometimes felt as if she
might be leaving a corner of her life too bare...

"*Three* kids," she said to her reflection in the
mirror over the sink as she dried her hands and
smoothed a stray strand of hair into the clip that held
it twisted in back. Gretchen had *three* kids. A whole
family. Of her own.

There couldn't be any long weekends or holidays or
downtime that Gretchen didn't know what she'd do
with herself.

And Gretchen had a husband, too. Along with her

career—though her career was more of a hobby than an all-consuming ambition.

But still, when Ally compared herself to her friend, she had to wonder if she was missing something. If she really had left a corner of her life too bare.

The image of Jake popped into her head just then. The way ideas did when she was decorating a room— as if he could be the perfect addition to the bare corner. As if he might complete the design.

No, no, no, that couldn't be!

"I'm not his type," she said aloud. "And even if *I* had a type—which I don't—he wouldn't be it."

Not only was he rooted in Chicago, there was also his friendship with her mother. Realistically, it didn't make sense that someone who had any kind of affinity for Estelle could be the man for Ally. She and Estelle were about as different as any two people could be, so if Jake Fox had anything in common with Estelle, it seemed to follow that he and Ally were *not* destined to hit it off. That ultimately, the way things began between them would be the rule, not the exception. Even if there had been—last night and today—times when it seemed as if they might be hitting it off.

What she needed to remember, she told herself, was that critical, controlling beginning with him. Because being critical and controlling was Estelle through and through.

"And I have to take that as a warning," she said firmly.

Okay, yes, maybe there was a corner of her life that needed a little something. But Jake Fox was not that little something. Regardless of what an appealing addition he could make.

"Sorry, Gretchen," she muttered in regards to her old friend's wish for her to be persuaded to move back to Chicago because of Jake Fox. "It's not going to happen."

And yet there was that melancholy feeling again...

Ally had no idea why or where it had come from.

But she didn't have time to analyze it.

Because just then she heard her name come over the hospital intercom, calling her to come to the emergency room immediately.

Chapter Five

"This was *good* news, Mother. *Really* good news."

"It's good news to you that there's something wrong with me? That I'll have to take pills the rest of my life?"

"It's good news that you didn't have a stroke or an aneurysm. That you don't have a brain tumor. That you won't even need to be tested for Alzheimer's. Compared to those possibilities, a thyroid problem is so much easier to deal with. All you'll have to do is take a pill and—"

"You know what I think of that—I hate pills! I hate medicine and the side effects and being a slave to it. I'm not living like that!"

Embarrassed, Ally knew several people were staring

at them in response to her mother's voice raised loud enough to be heard by nearby diners.

Ally pretended an interest in some of the worst food she'd ever tasted and let silence fall in hopes that Estelle would calm down if she did.

After Estelle's initial diagnosis, Jake had arranged for her to have an ultrasound to make sure her thyroid was not tumorous or enlarged or had any apparent disease. When the final conclusion was that it was merely treatably underactive, Jake had insisted on taking the three of them out for a celebration dinner. Estelle had given her opinion about fancy restaurants and overpriced food. She'd insisted they go to a buffet-style eatery where she had a two-for-one coupon and coffee was free to seniors. That was where they were having the discussion that seemed to disturb Jake far less than it did Ally.

"It's one pill a day for now, Estelle," he said calmly then. "Let's deal with that and not worry about anything else."

"I don't think I even have this thyroid thing."

"You do. I read all the reports myself," he said, not eating his dinner with any more enthusiasm than Ally was. "You have hypothyroidism—that means your thyroid has gotten sluggish. If you take the pill, most of the memory problems and confusion you've been having should go away or at least be considerably better. That unexplained weight gain you've been mad about will stop. And you'll be back to your sunny self."

He said that sarcastically, grinning when he did.

Ally waited for her mother to blast him for the remark.

But rather than exploding—the way her mother would have if Ally had said such a thing—Estelle laughed. "I've never been sunny and there's no pill that's going to change *that*."

"Let's let it do everything else, though," he urged as if he was enlisting her in a conspiracy.

Estelle took a bite of her pie and didn't agree or disagree.

Ally sat back in amazement.

Then Estelle took another tack. "I'm no good remembering to take pills like that—day in and day out. How is it going to help my memory if I can't remember to take them?"

"What if I get a small alarm clock that will go off at the same time every day?" Ally suggested. "You can keep the prescription bottle with it and when you hear the alarm, you'll know to take the pill."

"You want me to have a heart attack? Every day, out of the blue, some alarm blasting me?"

"I can get you something that plays music or has a tone that doesn't startle—"

Estelle flicked her hand as if she were angrily slapping away a fly.

"We'll figure something out," Jake said.

Ally wasn't sure why, but she had the sense that he had something else along those lines to talk to her about and didn't want to do it with Estelle there, so she conceded and suspended her attempts to find a solution.

"I suppose you'll be running back to California now,

won't you, Alice?" Estelle said then, her tone as sharp as a knife, the way it always was when she used Ally's given name.

"I do need to get back to work before too long, yes," Ally answered, very conscious of Jake being there for this. "But I'll make sure things are okay before I do."

"The grass is dying," Estelle said then, out of the blue, as if she were challenging Ally.

Estelle had been given a dose of her thyroid medication at the hospital, but Ally was reasonably sure it hadn't reversed the effects of her condition yet. So she assumed that the abrupt and erratic change of subject was another of Estelle's mental blips. And since she'd learned that it was easier to just go along with them, she said, "I know the grass was dying. I've been watering it since I got here."

"What about when you're not here?" Estelle demanded.

"Oh, we *are* still talking about my leaving."

"I can't keep up with things anymore. I'm alone, in case you've forgotten—"

"It isn't something I can ever forget," Ally said under her breath.

"The yard, the house—it's all on me. My problem. There'll be leaves in a few months and then there'll be snow—last year I got two notices from the mailman threatening not to deliver my mail and to give me a ticket if I didn't shovel the walks. But when it's deep I can't do it, I can't lift it."

Listening to her mother, Ally thought that these were

surely things that Jake had heard about from Estelle on the morning walks. Things that—since Ally hadn't been of help with any of them—had contributed to why he'd been so irritated with Ally before he'd even met her.

"I'm sorry," Ally said. "If you had told me—"

"It's fine. Never mind," Estelle snapped.

Ally had never been successful at pleasing or appeasing her mother. She shot a glance at Jake, hoping for guidance, but he only gave a sympathetic shrug of his eyebrows.

Ally looked back at Estelle and said, "I won't go home until I've taken care of everything."

"I don't need you to take care of me. Everything's been mine to do since—"

Ally saw the rage in her mother's eyes, in her expression, and she knew what Estelle was thinking, what she wanted to say.

But her mother stopped short and said only, "Everything's been mine to do since you *know* when. So leave tonight for all I care."

They were drawing outward stares now.

In a quiet, controlled voice, Ally tried again to calm her mother. "I'll make arrangements for the lawn, and for the leaves to be raked and hauled away when they fall. I'll see if I can have the landscaping people do snow removal, and if not, I'll find someone who will come whenever it snows—"

"And what if the furnace goes out? What about the rain gutters—the leaves get in there, too, you know.

They clog them up and then the ceiling leaks! And last year a branch on a tree across the street broke and went right through those people's roof—what about that? Milka had her husband to turn to. She has a son who came right over. But what would I do? Call you in California?"

It struck Ally then that what her mother was voicing was much like what she'd felt since arriving in Chicago—fear, frustration, being overwhelmed. And she understood that.

"Yes, no matter what happens, you can call me," she said firmly to get across to Estelle that she meant it.

But it still didn't ease her mother's anxiety. "What if you're in Italy—that's where you were last week, wasn't it? How could you fix my roof from there? You couldn't, that's how!"

Italy she remembers, Ally thought.

But desperate to quiet her mother, she made a rash decision and said, "You could come and live with me in California, then. We can sell the house. My condominium has three bedrooms, you'd have your own bathroom, the maintenance is all covered, and if something happened while I was away—"

"I was born and raised in Chicago! I've lived my whole life here! My friends are here! Everything I know is here! I'm not moving!" Estelle stopped herself and then said, "I think I'll wait for the two of you in front."

And out she went.

When Estelle was no longer in sight, Ally glanced at Jake again.

"That was quite a celebration," he said, clearly as taken aback as Ally.

"Welcome to my world," Ally muttered. Then, more pointedly, she said, "As a psychiatrist, isn't it your job to step into situations like this and calm people down or mediate or…*something?*"

Jake shook his head. "Things need to come out, people have to vent. It would have been better in a closed session rather than in a public place, but—" he shrugged "—she got it off her chest."

He said that very matter-of-factly, clearly undisturbed by the scene they'd been a part of.

Ally envied him his composure.

She picked up Estelle's purse from where it had fallen to the floor when her mother had stormed out. When she looked up again she found Jake watching her with compassion in his gray eyes.

"It's late," he said then. "It's been a long, stressful day all the way around. How about if I drop you and Estelle off—I'm sure she'll want to get to bed—and while you tuck her in, I'll swing by the liquor store. Then I'll come around to your place and we can wind down with a glass of wine and talk."

"I'd like that," Ally said wearily and maybe a little too eager for what he was offering.

But she was too wrung out to analyze that eagerness. Or to put up any resistance.

"White wine or red—what do you prefer?" he asked.

"At this point, anything with an alcohol content will do."

Jake glanced at the unappetizing food left on their plates. "Hard to say what should follow this."

"But we had a coupon," Ally managed a small joke.

Jake laughed. "Way to look on the bright side!" he teased her.

Surprisingly, it made Ally laugh along with him.

As she did, she thought that lifting her spirits and making her feel better at the worst of times was something he was getting good at.

And it made her realize she was beginning to like this man.

A lot. Perhaps more than she should.

Chapter Six

Ally's garage apartment was unbearably hot when she finally got upstairs. She, Jake and Estelle left the restaurant, and her mother had gone to bed. So she turned on the ceiling fan and the table fan to cool it off, then waited for Jake on the bottom step of the outdoor staircase that led to it, the corkscrew and wineglasses she'd taken from her mother's kitchen in hand.

"Has your landlady locked you out for failure to do your duty?" Jake asked in greeting when he came around the house and found her there a few minutes later.

"It's a good thing her room doesn't have a window facing back here—if she heard that she might consider it tonight," Ally answered, joking in return.

She'd been doing some deep breathing of the night air and she finally felt more relaxed than she had in the restaurant. Of course, it didn't hurt that her mother was out of the picture for the night and that she didn't have to worry about dealing with more from her until the next day.

It also didn't hurt that she was getting some quiet time alone with Jake again to finish out a day that would have been completely wretched if not for him.

Ally pointed upward toward her apartment. "My place was sealed tight until about ten minutes ago, so it's a sauna. I thought maybe we could sit out here instead. There's a glider—"

"It's nice right here," he said, sitting on the step beside her.

The wooden staircase was not wide and sharing one planked step made for close company. Jake's khaki-clad leg brushed the side of hers and she could smell the faint scent of his cologne.

Not that she even entertained the idea of changing anything. Even if she had convinced herself only hours earlier that he wasn't her type, he was right— this was nice…

He was carrying a brown paper sack and he set it on the ground between his feet.

"Wine," he announced as he took a bottle from the bag and handed it to her. "And crackers—just in case you might not have had enough dinner."

"I'll trade you—you open the wine and I'll open the crackers."

Jake accepted the deal and as he applied the cork-screw he said, "Did Estelle get to bed all right?"

"Just like nothing had ever happened. I think she might have forgotten everything she screamed about in the restaurant."

"I don't know about that," Jake said, pouring the wine into the glasses Ally held out. "Even if she forgot about the fit she threw, the facts are still the same—nothing she said wasn't true. She *has* been having all those problems around here and it *is* too much for her to handle alone now."

Ally sighed elaborately. "And I thought you weren't taking her side."

"No sides, just the facts. Plus, now there's medication she's going to need to take regularly," Jake reminded. "Things have changed for her, Ally, and she's scared. She can't do this alone."

Ally turned slightly so she could lean against the house's red brick wall and look at him in the faint glow of the light that was shining down on them from beside her apartment door. "I know that, Jake. But I live in L.A. My business is in L.A. I can do what I said I would in the restaurant, and try to get here more often—maybe even every couple of weeks—but I can't be here to force-feed her pills every day."

"There are houses that need decorating in Chicago," he suggested. But his observation sounded more theoretical than serious so it didn't push any buttons in her.

"I have to make a living, you know? Celebrities aren't my only clients. They aren't even the foundation of my business—they're the icing on the cake. If I left L.A., I'd have to bake a whole new cake."

"Would you if you could, though? Let's say something happened tomorrow that made you able to instantly have a new foundation here. Would you be *willing* to move?"

Ally thought about it. "I guess I'd consider it, yes. But even if that happened, there are contractual obligations I've already made that would take me away, so no matter what, I just can't be the sole solution."

He nodded as if he understood—which was an improvement over other times they'd had similar conversations about her responsibilities to her mother.

But after a sip of his wine and his second cracker he said, "The trouble is I just don't think Estelle can stay in this house on her own anymore."

"If the pills reverse her thyroid—"

"Even then. You heard what she said in the restaurant—"

"I think all of Chicago heard what she said in the restaurant."

"She has to have other living arrangements," he finished.

"Obviously she won't move to L.A. with me," Ally said wryly.

"Which leaves us with assisted living," he concluded. "Somewhere where she could be mainly on her own but without any upkeep and with at least a daily visit from staff to look in on her, make sure she's okay and taking her pills."

Again he was being logical, reasonable, matter-of-fact.

Ally waited for him to add something that criticized her for not providing that care of her mother. But it never came. Instead, after another cracker and more wine, he said, "I can go with you to check places out. Since I work so much with the elderly, I know the best— and worst—places out there."

"You'd do that?" she asked before she realized the words were going to come out, unable to keep the surprise from her voice.

"Sure. I want to see your mother in the best possible situation for her."

"Thank you," she said, appreciating what he was offering as well as the fact that he no longer seemed to be passing judgment.

"No problem," he answered. Then, as if he knew she'd been expecting flack from him, he added, "That's been my goal all along."

"I should get working on this as soon as possible," Ally said, both because it was true and to see if that provoked anything contrary from him.

But all he said was, "I'm free tomorrow afternoon. Bubby could probably come to stay with your mom— I think it's better if we go alone, figure out what's the best place and then present the idea to Estelle when we can lay out all the positives for her."

Ally nodded, once more pleasantly surprised by his agreeableness to all of this. But she decided not to rock the boat by pushing it any further than she had. Instead, as she sipped her wine and looked at him in the dim glow of the light, she couldn't help wondering about him and doing some pushing in another direction.

"How did you get so involved with geriatrics that you know the best living facilities?" she asked. "I remember you said Bubby put you to work at the senior center, but you said that she did that because you have so much to do with the elderly anyway—how did it happen that you have so much to do with them in the first place?"

Jake shrugged. "Working with seniors fills a void for me."

"You said before that you don't have any family—is that the void? Did you lose your own parents and replace them with your seniors?"

"Not exactly. I lost my parents when I was three, so I really almost never had a family," he said very solemnly.

"Your parents passed away when you were only a child?"

"They were killed in a convenience-store robbery."

"Oh, Jake, I'm so sorry. But…you didn't have any family to take care of you?" she ventured, hoping she was misunderstanding.

"Not a soul. No grandparents, no siblings, and both my parents were only children, so no aunts or uncles. Nothing."

"Oh," she said, stunned and working to adjust her vision of him because this was so much different than anything she'd imagined. "So you were…"

"Thrown into the system."

"Which means what, exactly?"

"It means that the first thing that was tried was to find adoptive parents. But most people want newborns and a three-year-old is not a newborn."

"It's not much more than a baby, though," she said, her heart wrenching at the idea of a child so small, so defenseless, being unwanted.

"That may be, but it still meant I wasn't a great candidate for adoption. So the only other option was to put me into foster care, where I was until I became a teenager. Then I was in several group homes until I was eighteen."

"Were you in one foster home until the group homes?"

"Oh, no," he said as if it had been far from that—and not a happy situation. "I can't even tell you how many foster homes I was in. I'd be with one family for a while—long enough to get settled in and start hoping it would be where I was for good—and then something would happen. The foster parents would decide they didn't want to be a foster family anymore, or there would be a work transfer, or they'd have a new baby of their own, or you name it—I was moved for just about any reason you can think of and then some. Foster homes aren't permanent arrangements—that's why adoption would have been better. As it was, the longest I stayed anywhere was a year."

Ally ached at the image of him as a little boy, never knowing the warmth of family.

Of course, *she'd* had family, and it had been far from perfect.

"Did you form *any* attachments?"

Jake shook his head. "I learned early not to count on anybody being in my life forever. Social workers changed, foster families changed, schools changed— definitely no fixtures."

"And you went from foster homes to group homes? I'm not even sure I know what group homes are."

"The ones I was in were suburban houses that Social Services owned. Eight to ten kids around the same age lived in them at any given time. We had round-the-clock adult supervision, but the staff didn't live in, they just did eight-hour shifts then handed off to the next person—like at a nursing home or a jail—"

"*Was* it like a jail or a nursing home?"

"A little of both actually," he said with a laugh, even though it didn't seem funny to Ally.

"Group homes get a mix of kids," he explained. "A lot of conduct-disorder kids, some who have just come out of detention facilities or rehab, and some who had to be removed from their homes because of abuse or neglect. But along with housing, it's important to teach those same kids the skills to get them out on their own when the state cuts them loose at eighteen."

"So you were there for all those reasons."

"Well, also because when I hit puberty I became a kind of rebel without a cause and got into some trouble that ended my foster-care days."

"You—Mr. Make-Sure-I-Do-What's-Right—got into trouble?" she said, finding it hard to believe of him.

"I did," he said, again with a laugh. "I went through a what-the-hell phase."

"Meaning?"

"Meaning, what the hell difference did it make if I went to school? Or swiped cigarettes and booze from my foster parents' store to sell myself? Or what the hell difference did it make if I drove without a license? That kind of what-the-hell phase that got me kicked out of foster care and thrown into juvie for three months, after which I was put into group homes as one of the conduct-disorder kids."

She would never have guessed this of him. "How did you turn all that around and end up being a doctor?"

"I came into contact with a lot of kids worse off than I was. Kids who *couldn't* get through school. Who couldn't cope. Kids with—"

"More serious emotional and mental problems," Ally finished for him, remembering his telling her that he'd grown up around a lot of people like that.

"Yes," he confirmed.

"But that was before you were in therapy yourself?"

"Actually, some of the therapy was in the group homes—everybody was required to go through counseling sessions. Plus, as a conduct-disorder kid I had to have outside therapy, too. The sessions at the group homes with the other kids was where I discovered I was good at reasoning with my peers, at problem solving, at helping them work through things, but it was the outside therapy that made me start to think about doing it as a job."

"So helping kids you lived with was what turned you around?"

"It did. I started school again, went to summer classes to make up what I'd missed so I could graduate on time. Then I worked my way through college and survived on student loans to go to med school. And here I am."

Ally was impressed. "But given what that ambition came from, I would have thought you'd end up working with kids, not with their grandparents."

"I work with all age groups. But I do particularly like the give-and-take with the older people who I didn't get a chance to have in my life growing up. When I'm with them it's like being surrounded by a whole bunch of grandparents now."

"Some of them nice and some of them surly," Ally remarked, thinking again about their dinner.

Jake laughed. "Yeah, but I enjoy the surly ones, too."

"I hope you're right. But after tonight I just don't know..." Ally said with a sigh. "And speaking of grumps, do you think I'll have to hypnotize Mother to move her to assisted living?"

He laughed again. "We might save that as a backup plan."

Ally hated to think what sort of scene she'd be in for and it made her feel very weary again. Weary enough to show it by grumbling and collapsing forward for dramatic effect. But her forehead landed on Jake's knee, and it was only after she got there that she realized that it was probably inappropriate.

Wine, little to eat, stress and fatigue—she knew that's what had gotten her there without having thought it through in advance. But now that that's where she was, she recognized that she'd gotten herself into something she shouldn't have.

Except that before she could sit up again, he began to gently massage the back of her neck.

"Let's just find a place first and then deal with telling Estelle," he advised, but in a tone that was as quiet and intimate as his touch as he worked her bare nape with a gentle but firm caress.

"At least now I know not to talk to her about it in a public place," Ally joked, her own voice an octave lower.

Jake laughed yet again, a sound that came from deeper in his chest this time, a sexy sort of rumble that let her know she wasn't the only one of them being affected.

Too affected, maybe, because things were beginning to roil in her that didn't belong, that shouldn't be happening in this relationship that had no future.

And yet when she did make herself sit up again, Jake's hand went with her, remaining cupped around the back of her neck, not letting her go too far away.

In fact, she ended up with her face only inches from his.

He was looking into her eyes, searching them as if he could see beneath the surface, and in that instant everything else fell away except the simple attraction that

Ally felt for him. The same attraction that she knew instinctively he felt for her.

And that was when he tilted his head and leaned forward to kiss her.

Ever since the night before, she'd done a lot more thinking about what kissing Jake might be like—not that she'd wanted to know firsthand or even understood why she'd thought so much about it. But in thinking so much about it she'd told herself that he wouldn't be any good at it. That a kiss from him would likely be by the book, stiff, succinct.

It was *nothing* like that. Oh, could the man kiss! His breath was warm against her cheek, his lips were parted the perfect amount, he knew how to move, how to engage, how to dominate just enough to draw her in and persuade her to kiss him in return.

And she did. It was a kiss too good not to enjoy, not to give back so it would go on a while longer, so she could have the full taste of lips that were firm and soft at the same time, the full mingling of his wine-sweet breath with hers, the full feeling of connecting with Jake Fox…

But then his mouth was gone and his hand slipped away.

"I should go," he said.

Because he'd kissed her? Or just because he should go?

"I suppose so," Ally agreed. What else was she going to do, invite him upstairs in an impulsive reaction to a simple kiss that had had more than a simple impact on her?

And even if that completely uncalled-for thought occurred to her, there was no way she was going to do it. That would have been inappropriate!

Jake handed her the wineglass and stood. "I'll call Bubby and then check with you after I find out if she can come over and sit with your mom," he was saying into Ally's confusion of thoughts and feelings and the lingering sensation of his mouth on hers.

"Okay," she said.

"And then we'll do some assisted-living hunting."

Ally nodded, coming back to earth a little more with the reminder of that.

But not all the way back to earth.

Because even as Jake said good-night, got up and left her sitting there on the bottom step, a part of Ally was still engulfed in that kiss.

That kiss—along with what she'd learned about him tonight—that had somehow shined an entirely new light on Jake and made her see him very differently.

That had made her see him as more than the guy who had bullied her into coming home, as more than her mother's friend.

Suddenly she saw a great-looking, personable, intelligent, interesting man who she was enjoying getting to know. Who she was enjoying spending time with. Who she wanted to get to know even more.

And who she could have kissed until the sun came up…

Chapter Seven

"Mother? What are you doing?" Ally asked Estelle when she went into the house Sunday morning and found her mother looking through a ragged shoe box full of old photographs at the kitchen table.

"I couldn't open the front door to get my paper—yesterday when I did that, you came running like the house was on fire. And I like to have something to look at while I drink my coffee, so I got out my pictures."

While Ally had finished dressing she'd listened through the intercom and had heard Estelle up and about. But since Ally hadn't heard anything alarming, she hadn't rushed over this morning. She'd forgotten about her mother's newspaper.

Rather than going out to get it off the front porch now, Ally was curious about the photographs, so she poured herself a cup of coffee and joined her mother at the table.

"I've never seen these," she said, leaning to one side to look at the snapshot Estelle was staring at.

"It's my special box," Estelle said, sounding nostalgic.

Ally felt a bit…slighted. "Do you want to be alone?"

"It's all right," Estelle said amiably. Then she handed Ally the picture. It was a black-and-white photograph of a high-school-age Estelle in a cheerleader's uniform. She was one of four girls who all wore the same uniform and were posed with megaphones.

"You were a cheerleader?"

"When I was a senior…" Estelle chuckled wryly. "A different kind of senior than they call me now."

Ally laughed. "Did you cheer for Daddy?" She knew her parents had met in high school and married two weeks after they'd graduated but not anything more than that.

"Oh, no, your father didn't play sports. I cheered for Cubby Grissom."

"I heard Daddy mention that name, didn't I?"

"Probably. They were best friends," Estelle said, handing Ally two more photos to point out Cubby Grissom. In one of them he had his arms affectionately around the young Estelle.

After seeing that, Ally raised her eyebrows over her cup as she took a sip of her coffee. "You went out with Daddy's best friend?"

"I had such a crush on Cubby!" Estelle confided.

"And he was crazy about me. At Mitchie's and my wedding, when we walked back up the aisle, Cubby was in the last church pew with big tears in his eyes because I was marrying Mitchie instead of him."

"Mother!" Ally pretended to chastise. "I didn't know you were a heartbreaker!"

"Only Cubby's."

It was rare that Ally had the opportunity to talk to Estelle as if they were friends, and she relished the moment.

"How did you end up marrying Daddy?" Ally asked as she was shown wedding pictures that hadn't made it into the album.

"No one could believe it," Estelle said. "Not even me. Not after the way Mitchie and I started out, that's for sure. We fought and argued and at first I thought he was the biggest jackass…" Again Estelle said that with nostalgia in her voice, but now with humor, too. "I didn't like him at all. He was just a friend of Cubby's I had to put up with."

Sort of like Jake, Ally thought. Initially he'd just been the jackass she'd argued with and hadn't liked but had had to put up with because he was her mother's friend…

"What did you argue about?" she asked Estelle.

"Oh, silly things—who we liked in school and who we didn't. What teachers were good and which ones weren't. Movies, music, books, just everything."

"So how did you go from that to *marrying* him?" Not that Ally thought for a single second that she was going to go from a similar beginning with Jake to that. She was just curious.

"I don't know…" Estelle said wistfully. "We were together a lot of the time because of Cubby and for some reason things just started to fall into place—we started to joke about how much we disagreed, he made me laugh… Something just sparked."

Like Jake's kiss last night…

"And then," Estelle concluded, "I didn't like Cubby anymore—well, I still liked him as a friend, but the crush just went away—and Mitchie and I ended up being like two halves of a whole."

Which had always been what Ally had believed of her parents—that one without the other was incomplete. Something she couldn't fathom ever being true of her.

Estelle took another picture from the old shoe box and grinned. "Niagara Falls—that's where we went on our honeymoon. That was where we decided that we wanted to travel all we could. That that would be the kind of life we'd have together."

"Really?" Ally said. Niagara Falls didn't seem like such an exotic trip that it would inspire dreams of travel. Plus, this was the first she'd ever heard of her parents deciding that should be the goal of their married life. "I don't remember you ever going anywhere," she added.

"Traveling was all we worked for," Estelle said, beginning to pull out snapshot after snapshot of herself and Ally's father in various touristy locations around the country. "Mitchie went to work in construction, I got a job in a fabric store, and we'd cut corners and save everything we could for our vacation every year. We were going to see the whole country!"

"It looks like you almost did," Ally commented, because there were photographs of her parents at Mount Rushmore, at the Grand Canyon, at Hoover Dam, at Yellowstone and Yosemite, even hiking in the Rocky Mountains.

"Was this why you weren't planning to have kids? So you could travel?" Ally asked. She'd known that her parents had not intended to have a family, but she'd always assumed the reason was because they'd been so much in love that they hadn't wanted anything but each other.

But like her comment about never remembering them traveling, Estelle didn't answer this question either. She seemed lost in memories and reluctant to emerge from them.

"We went every year until we turned forty," she said instead. "And then we started to talk about wanting to see more of the world, wanting an adventure, wanting to know what it was like to live in Europe."

"You wanted to *move* there?"

"Not forever, but we thought if we saved enough money by not going anywhere for a few years, we could maybe stay six months. And if we had that long, we could travel and live for a little while wherever we felt like it. It would have been so nice…"

"But you never did that?"

"No. Just when we were going to, I got pregnant."

"Oh."

"Then all the money had to go for doctors and baby furniture and bottles and things," Estelle said emotionlessly, merely stating fact. "And after that everything was different. It cost more for day care or to hire a babysitter than I could make working, so I needed to stay home. We barely got by on Mitchie's wages alone with three mouths to feed, and that was that."

Estelle gathered up her pictures as if *that was that* for looking at them, too. As she did she said, "Now you travel, Alice, and I just hear about it."

Ally was surprised that there was no resentment in her mother's voice. But still she felt guilty, as if she'd unwittingly gotten to live a portion of life her mother had wanted but been denied because of her.

"I had no idea," she said.

"There wasn't any reason for you to know. Once you were on the way we made our decision not to stop it. Mitchie said it must have been in the grand design that we have you so we should. That we could travel again later."

Except later hadn't come because her father had died when Ally was twelve.

"I'm sorry," she said softly.

Estelle didn't respond. In fact, the remark didn't even seem to register.

"Maybe you and I could take a trip," Ally added. "You could come to Italy the next time I need to go. We could arrange to stay for a few weeks, maybe go to Paris and London—"

"Oh, I don't need that now," Estelle said. "Just this is enough—you, here."

That gave Ally pause. "It is?"

"I'm glad when you visit," her mother said, and it sounded genuine. "I wish you would more often. Or move back, even—that would be nice."

"It *would?*"

"You probably don't think so, but I do. There's so much of Mitchie in you—that was hard for me to see for so long after we lost him. But now it's like getting two for the price of one. And you know I like a bargain." Estelle smiled at her own joke and Ally managed to, too.

"You're a good girl, Alice," her mother announced as she stood and took her box of pictures with her. "I'm proud of you."

Then she walked out of the kitchen, leaving Ally with the biggest surprise of this entire visit—praise from her mother and a warm feeling to go with it.

Chapter Eight

Ally was sitting on the lawn swing late Sunday evening, watching Jake come out of the back door of her mother's house. He was in profile to her, holding the screen door open with his oh-so-terrific derriere as he bid her mother good-night. Then he stepped off the small landing and let the screen close, turning to cross the yard to her, carrying two glasses.

He was wearing jeans and a plain T-shirt, and he still looked outstanding bathed in the light from the fixture beside the door.

"The last two margaritas," he announced, handing one glass to her when he reached her.

"Thanks," Ally said, making room for him to join her

on the dated lawn furniture that creaked and slid backward with his weight when he sat beside her.

Ally sipped her drink and watched the lights go off in her mother's kitchen. She'd said good-night to Estelle moments before when her mother had announced that she was going to bed and Jake had followed her inside to refill his and Ally's glasses.

Jake turned in her direction and she could feel his gaze steadily on her. It seemed to add to the warm summer air around them and Ally was glad she was wearing her lightest-weight jeans and only a thin scoop-neck T-shirt.

"When you clam up, Rogers, you really clam up," he said before he took a drink of his own.

Ally smiled at him. "I haven't clammed up," she answered defensively, casting him a glance out of the corner of her eye.

"You've been quiet all day," Jake insisted.

He was right, she had been. Luckily he'd done most of the talking at the half-dozen assisted-living facilities they'd visited that afternoon. Jake had asked questions she hadn't even thought to and made sure she knew everything she needed to know. Then they'd come home and he'd suggested a backyard barbecue for which he'd done most of the work, with Estelle pitching in with more enthusiasm than Ally had seen from her mother in a long time. Ally had been able to go on wallowing in the thoughts that had kept her in their grip since that morning's talk with her mother.

"You and Mother seem to get into your own rhythm," she said as if that explained her not saying much all day and evening.

"Even when we tried to get you to talk tonight you weren't into it. What's up?"

She sipped more of the tart beverage. "I just have a lot on my mind today."

"Such as?"

"Such as who knew my mother could make such a mean margarita," Ally joked.

Jake laughed, toasted her with his glass and enjoyed another taste of the beverage. But he seemed determined not to be detoured.

"Were you put off by the places we looked at today?" he asked.

"No, they were all nice enough. Not luxury living, but nice." She repeated what she'd said as they'd driven home when the conversation had stalled so as not to alert Estelle to what they'd done while they'd been out.

"And yet you hardly said two words and didn't make even tentative commitments to any of them," Jake pointed out. "Do you want to see more of them?"

"No."

"So what's up?" he said again.

Ally shrugged. "I've just been thinking a lot today— and tonight—about how important it was to my mother to keep this house after my dad died. How she said more times than I can remember that the house was our security. That it was all she had…"

"And now she'd be losing it," Jake guessed.

"Well, yes. And even if she hasn't been doing so well at keeping up with the lawn, she still has her flower gardens and her few vegetable plants—she wouldn't have any of that in assisted living."

"No, she wouldn't."

"Plus, the places are all far from the senior center and the park, and from those of her friends who live around here. She's only driving when she has to, so she probably wouldn't be able to walk with you guys, or get to the senior center. She could lose touch with her friends—"

Jake had sobered considerably. "She wouldn't lose complete touch with her friends—they all still have telephones and they make an effort to include even those of them who move into assisted living or with family members. But you're right—when they aren't close by, they don't see as much of each other."

"It's sad and it's all the same reasons she gave for not wanting to come and live with me in L.A.," Ally said. "They're valid reasons, too—I'd hate it if I were her, it doesn't seem good for her, and I don't want to be the one who takes more away from her."

"So, you be the one to move, then. Pack up and come back to Chicago."

"We already went through that—it isn't as if I can ask my boss for a transfer to the Illinois branch," she said. "But that doesn't mean that I don't feel bad that I can't just do that."

"If it were an option, would you?" he asked, sounding as if it gave him an idea of some kind.

Ally didn't know what idea it might have given him, but she did think about the what-if of having a choice. "I don't know if I would do it or not. It would be a hard decision. But it doesn't matter because it isn't an option."

"Which again brings us back to assisted living."

Ally sighed wryly. "And what a great choice that is. I ruined some of her life by being born, and she's spent my adult years watching me do what she wanted to and couldn't because she'd had me, and now I can strike one final blow, too."

"Wow!" Jake said, rearing back. "What's all that?"

"The truth. Some of it I just learned this morning."

"Sounds like a big load to be carrying around," he said.

Ally groaned theatrically. "Ugh! Don't treat me like one of your patients."

He grinned. "Okay, where the hell did all that come from and what are you talking about?"

Ally laughed. "Better," she judged even as she debated whether or not to bare her soul to him.

Things were different between them now. He didn't seem like an adversary the way he had then. And he was a good listener and she was really in need of unloading, so she decided to do that soul-baring after all.

"My parents had not planned to ever have kids— that's why I'm the age of most of Mother's friends' grandchildren rather than their children. I was an unwelcome surprise."

"Do you know you were unwelcome or is that just something you've felt?"

"Oh, I know it. Even before she told me, Mother kept me at arm's length and made me feel like a stray cat that had just been given a home out of necessity."

"Come on," Jake said in disbelief.

"I'm serious. She and my father adored—and I mean *adored*—each other. They were closer and meant more to each other, were more important to each other and more kindred spirits, than any two people I've ever met. And I always had a strong sense that I was butting into that. My dad put effort into hiding it—he went out of his way to spend time with me and really tried to be interested in what I liked to do. Which was nice—I felt closer to him because of that. But the flip side of it was that Mother resented it."

"What made you think that?"

"She'd say that Daddy was spread too thin because of me. She was always aggravated with how needy I was. Or she'd tell me I was too demanding."

"Ouch."

Ally shrugged as if it hadn't been as hurtful as it had. "But this morning I found out, how much my being born had changed for her and the strangest thing happened—for the first time I put myself in her shoes and even though a part of me still resented the way she handled things, another part of me understood. I kept thinking that if, right now, I was where she'd been and suddenly all my plans, everything I wanted, had to be put on hold for some unforeseen reason, and I had to share a man I was blissfully happy not sharing, I'd probably resent it, too. And considering that now she's had to watch me go on to have those things she was denied? I ended up feeling guilty."

"You can't feel guilty because you've been successful and built your own life. It isn't as if you won't have your own disappointments to deal with."

"Still, it was because of me that her life played out the way it did—"

"I understand what you're saying, Ally. And what you're feeling. But you're doing the best you can for Estelle now. Using your advantages to help her in the present and the future to make her life better are productive ways to pay her back for whatever sacrifices she might have made. But guilt for being born?" He grasped the crown of her head with his fingertips and then pulled his hand away. "I'm absolving you of that."

Ally laughed again. "Thank you," she said.

"You're welcome," he answered as if he'd actually done something.

He finished his drink and set the glass on the swing's platform. Then he sat back again and looked at her.

"It seems I'm still missing some of the picture, though," he said then. "What was your father's role while all this was going on?"

That put a new damper on Ally's mood. "That's something I can't *ever* make up for," she said, bending forward to deposit her own glass under the swing.

"But we've come this far, you might as well take me the rest of the way," he cajoled, again stretching his arm along the cushion so he could fiddle with her hair, rubbing a strand of it between his fingers as if it were silk.

Ally took a deep breath and sighed, deciding that since she had come this far she might as well tell him the whole story. Even if it was something she'd never confided in anyone.

"When I was twelve I left my bicycle in the driveway behind my father's car—"

"Something just about every kid does at least once," he said as if he was contradicting her dire tone.

"My dad didn't see it and backed out over it—"

"Again, something that happens."

"And doesn't seem like a big deal, does it?" she agreed. "Except that apparently some part of the bike pierced his tire. He didn't notice it and the tire went flat on the highway. My dad had to change it and while he did, he was hit by another car."

Jake's whole face scrunched into a sympathetic frown. "That's how he died, isn't it?" he finished for her because she stalled before getting to that point.

She nodded her confirmation. "That was when I found out for sure that I'd been an unwelcome surprise. My dad dying was more awful for me than I can tell you. But for Mother? He was her other half. When we found out he was dead she just lost it. She kind of went crazy. She told me it was my fault—as if I didn't know that. She said it was bad enough that she'd had to share him with me for twelve years but she couldn't believe that my dad had been taken from her and *I* was what she was left with. She told me straight out that she'd never wanted me, that she wished she'd never had me, that if she hadn't he would have still been alive."

It was too awful and ugly a memory to go into any further and Ally stopped.

"You're right, she did go crazy," Jake said softly. "Grief can do that. But what gets said in a time like that—"

"Can still be the truth," Ally said before he could tell her her mother hadn't meant it.

"It did damage," Jake conceded.

"I knew after that that I hadn't been imagining what I'd thought before—that I was an intrusion and that she resented it. And even though she never said it again, I knew from then on that she blamed me for my father's death. The rift between us just got wider after that. Everything was so much harder without my dad around. Plus, Mother had to support the two of us and she wasn't educated or experienced enough to get a job that paid well, so she had to work long hours, she was always tired—"

"And there had to be a lot of grieving and depression over a loss like that. For both of you."

"She definitely wasn't happy-go-lucky. And the financial problems made it worse. Keeping the house became such a big thing—it wasn't easy for her to go on making the mortgage payments, but she was determined. It was like her lifeline or something…"

Jake motioned with his chin in the direction of the

garage apartment. "And you ended up living there instead of in the house with her?"

"Like I said, things between us just got more strained. As soon as I was old enough, I found an after-school job so I could contribute to the household income. Around that same time I started to think about the space above the garage. Daddy had been working on it before he died to turn it into an apartment. He'd gotten about half finished—it was wired for electricity and heat, the plumbing was in, and he'd even collected those old appliances and cupboards from garage sales. Anyway, I started to think that maybe I could do the rest of the work. I saved the money I wasn't putting in on the family budget so I could buy the materials. I checked out how-to books from the library, I asked a lot of questions at the hardware store, and I managed to finish the apartment. Then I really got into painting it, decorating it, adding throw rugs and my own touches—"

"Was that when you realized you wanted to be a decorator?"

"It was," she said. "And when I was finished with it, I just moved up there."

"Estelle didn't mind?"

"We never really talked about it. I started to stay up there more and more, and she seemed to accept it. My being in the apartment more than in the house made it easier for us to just sort of coexist. We had meals together. Mother kept tabs on me. I had curfews and rules and all of that, but when I was home, I was in the apartment and she was in the house, and that's how it was. I stayed through college, and when I graduated, I applied for a job with a design firm that came to my school to recruit. The firm was in California, so with the job, came the move, and that's where I went."

"And you've never tried to heal all those old wounds?"

She shook her head. "I think it's better to just move on."

"Sometimes that *is* better," he agreed. "But sometimes people come to me because they've taken that route and the parent has died and they feel differently. They wish they hadn't just gone on. It can be tougher to work through those things then."

Ally cast him another sidelong glance. "What did I tell you about treating me like a patient?"

He grinned sheepishly. "Believe me, this isn't a therapy session for me," he answered, still stroking her hair.

"I'm sorry, Ally," he said then.

Ally turned her head enough to look at him more squarely as his hand went back to the seat cushion.

Disappointed, she pretended not to notice. "You're sorry for treating me like a patient?" she asked, confused.

"No, I'm sorry for my own mishandling of getting you here. *I* blamed you, too, and I was out of line. I guess I always want to believe that any family is better than none and I like Estelle, so I thought you weren't appreciating what you have in her. But now..." His hand returned to cup the back of her head. "A lot of people would have just left her hanging out to dry and figured it was what she had coming, but that isn't what you've done. I admire that, and I'd say Estelle is lucky to have you."

Ally grinned at him. "Praise from her this morning and from you tonight—this really is my day."

"We should come up with something better to do than looking at assisted-living facilities on Ally Rogers Day," he joked.

"I think it's too late for a parade," she countered with a laugh.

"Guess I'll just have to think of something else," he said with sexy insinuation in his voice.

He leaned toward her then, pausing a split second with his face close to hers, giving her the opportunity to stop him if she didn't want a repeat of last night's kiss.

But that kiss of the night before had stayed with her during the last twenty-four hours. So she merely smiled a tiny, coy smile in that instant before his mouth touched hers.

She raised one of her hands to his face as his lips parted and enticed hers to do the same. She pressed her other hand to the wall of his chest, feeling the hard muscles just beneath his T-shirt. His free arm came around her to hold her, to pull her nearer as his tongue began to toy with hers. Mouths opened wider and that kiss became something a whole lot more involving, more intimate.

Ally's right hand slipped from his face around to the back of his neck, testing the coarse texture of his hair. Her left went from his chest to his back where she pressed her palm to the expanse of his broad shoulders and closed what scant distance there still was between them so that her breasts barely brushed his chest.

But still, more than anything, it was that kiss that held her attention. Deep, plundering, and ripe with passion, it wasn't the kiss of a contained, controlled professional, but the smolderingly sexy kiss of a hot-blooded man with nothing on his mind but her.

Somehow she'd turned enough to be sideways on the swing and he was easing her backward. And she was willing to go. To lie down, to have him lie beside her, to go on and on kissing and touching and who-knew-what-else.

But that was when Ally remembered where they were, that her mother was just inside the house, that Estelle could come down to the kitchen at any moment for a glass of water and see them there in the backyard, going at it like two teenagers.

And as much as she didn't want to stop this—and, oh boy, did she not want to stop this—she brought both of her palms to Jake's chest and gave him just enough of a nudge to get the message across that they should cool it.

He was clearly no more eager than she was, because he went on kissing her slightly more chastely for a few minutes longer. Then there was a break, a kiss, another break and another kiss before the third break brought a heavy sigh from him and he sat up straighter, taking her with him.

"Is the porch light going to flash to warn us to knock

it off?" he asked in a low voice that let her know he knew what had been going through her mind.

"I'm afraid it could at any time," she said. "And believe me, you don't want that. It comes with a raging Estelle saying she won't have anything like *that* going on right under her nose."

Jake grinned a crooked, devilishly evil grin. "Anything like what?" He played dumb.

"Anything like French kissing and ruining my reputation—she's always been very keen on my Reputation with a capital R."

"Or she could worry about you ruining my Reputation-with-a-capital-R," Jake suggested.

Ally laughed. "That's probably more likely."

Taking his cue, he stood to leave. "I better take off before you get caught corrupting me."

Ally stood, too—but not before drinking in the sight of him once more, towering above her with that perfectly proportioned body and that slightly wayward mane of hair silhouetted against the porch light they'd been joking about. And like the previous night, she had a flashing thought of asking him up to her place to start that kiss all over again. To take it even further...

For the second time she managed to refrain, but it didn't escape her that resisting it tonight was a struggle.

"I'll walk you out," she offered.

"Nah, my keys are in my pocket. I'll just go around the house."

He laid a hand to the side of her face and kissed her

again, then said, "Don't forget tomorrow night. Dinner at my friend Nina's with her family and Bubby."

It was the invitation Bubby had extended to all of them when Ally and Jake had returned home today. Bubby and her granddaughter wanted to cook for them.

"I guess so," Ally said uncertainly.

"I'll pick you two up," he added.

She noted that he didn't ask if it was okay. Not that it wasn't. At that moment it was just a good thing he wasn't ordering her to do more, because she doubted she could have denied him.

"We'll be here," she said.

Another kiss. This one a little hotter than the one that had preceded it, sending the message that there were still things churning in him the same way they were still churning in her.

But then that was it. Jake whispered a husky good-night and left.

Ally watched him go, her gaze dropping from wide shoulders to narrow waist to hips and a to-die-for rear end that swayed just enough with each stride of long, thick legs...

Only when he disappeared around the side of the house did she realize that she'd been holding her breath.

She released it, but as if that had been keeping her bottled up, when the air went out of her other things were set free.

Namely a terrible yearning to be back in Jake's arms with his mouth on hers.

And she couldn't help wondering where things might have gone from there if she hadn't stopped him.

Because the man did have a talent for starting on a sour note and ending on a sweet one.

And the sweet notes were getting better and better.

Chapter Nine

"Don't tell me you aren't interested in seeing my bat mitzvah pictures for the hundredth time," Nina Hanson teased Jake when he joined his old friend and her husband in their kitchen Monday evening.

Ally and Estelle were in the other room chatting with Bubby, who was thrilled to have a new audience for her show-and-tell.

"Not that you weren't a cute kid," Jake answered, "but I *have* seen those pictures often enough for them to be burned into my brain."

"Poor Ally," Nina commiserated, laughing, too. "I should go in there and save her."

"I wanted to talk to you guys about her," Jake said

before his friend could leave the kitchen. "Although David is really who I need to talk to about her, so if you don't want in on it, Nina—"

"Oh, no, you're not getting rid of me if you're talking about Ally—this dinner was designed for me to meet her and find out everything I can about her and what's going on with the two of you. I'm not skipping anything."

Jake and Nina spoke on the phone almost every day, so they'd touched base more than once since the Friday-night dinner. He was well aware of Nina's suspicions that he was attracted to Ally. So far he'd been skirting the issue and he continued to ignore it now. Instead, in a mock aside to her husband, he said, "I figured that would keep her around."

Then he got to the point.

"Nina has been telling me about the problems with the two Taka hotels."

David sighed, clearly frustrated. "Things are bad at both sites, that's for sure. I got an anonymous e-mail today suggesting that our decorator is actually on Drake Thatcher's payroll. Whoever sent it claims that Thatcher has promised Riki—Riki is the designer's name, just Riki, no last name," David interrupted himself to explain before going on. "Anyway, the claim is that Thatcher has promised Riki the decorator job for the Thatcher Group hotels if Riki does enough damage to us. And he's done plenty—all the interiors on the San Francisco project are so far behind that it's going to be a killer to catch up. It looks like Tom and Helen will have to beat the bushes for a new designer."

"That's what I wanted to talk to you about," Jake said. "Nina told me you might be looking for a new decorator and I may have a solution for you."

David's surprise was apparent. "No kidding? How?"

Jake poked his thumb over his shoulder, in the direction of the living room where Bubby was showing family photographs. "Ally," he said simply.

David Hanson's eyebrows arched even higher. "I know she's a designer, and she lives in L.A., which could be convenient for the San Francisco site. But we want to hire one person to do all the hotels and we need someone based in Chicago. Granted, in the final stages the decorator spends a lot of time on-site, but otherwise it's better to have someone Helen can work closely with, and in order for that to happen, they need to be here."

Helen was Helen Taka-Hanson, David's sister-in-law. After the death of her husband, she had been instrumental in putting together the merger that had brought Hanson Media into business with Taka Corporation, a Japanese conglomerate. In the process she'd also helped bring the Hanson family together again. Since then she'd gained another husband—Mori Taka—as well as guided the family into launching the new hotel chain, and she continued to play a pivotal role in the business.

"Working out of Chicago is actually why I wanted to talk to you about Ally. A client as big as the Taka hotel chain would give her the chance to relocate."

"Would she be willing to do that?" Nina asked.

"I can't say for sure—"

"But you're hoping," Nina goaded.

Jake didn't take the bait. He merely repeated himself. "Ally understands that her mother needs her, only she says that with her clients primarily on the West Coast, she can't move because she'd be leaving her livelihood behind. That's when I started to think that this might solve everyone's problems—you would get a new decorator in a hurry, Ally would get a substantial foundation to establish her business in Chicago, and Estelle would get Ally close by."

"Not to mention that you would get Ally close by, too." This from Nina again.

David thought for a minute and said, "You could have something there. Of course, the decision would be up to Helen—this is her field, not mine—but I can talk to her in the morning before my plane takes off. If she's interested she can call Nina and between the two of you, you can put Ally in touch with Helen."

Jake nodded, satisfied that he'd set the wheels into motion.

"I haven't said anything about this to Ally, though," he said. "And it's probably better if we don't until you talk to Helen—"

"You haven't discussed this with Ally?" Nina exclaimed in disbelief. "Don't you think you're overstepping your bounds to be doing this *without* talking to her first?"

"I wouldn't want to get Ally's or Estelle's hopes up if Helen has her heart set on someone else," Jake reasoned. "Estelle would be disappointed and Ally could get her feelings hurt, and I don't want either of those things to happen if they don't have to."

David looked to Nina, who shrugged in what appeared to be reluctant concession to that. Then he said to Jake, "Helen is out tonight, but I'll leave her a message to let her know I need to talk to her first thing tomorrow, before she gets any further with the search for a new designer. If she isn't interested in Ally, Ally won't have to know and feel rejected."

"Or realize what you two big men are doing behind her back," Nina muttered. "And then no more business," she warned as her husband headed for the telephone.

"Then no more business," David agreed.

As David began to make his call, Nina and Jake moved into the dining room. But they could see into the living room from there and Bubby was still showing family photographs.

"I say we wait here until they're finished," Nina said.

"That gets my vote," Jake agreed. They went to the sideboard where trays of appetizers were already showing a dent, and helped themselves so it wasn't too obvious that they were avoiding the pictures.

"I really like Ally," Nina said as they nibbled bruschetta. "Which is another reason I think you should talk to her about this job *before* putting her name on the table."

That barely registered with Jake, because he couldn't keep from looking over his old friend's head at the lady in question.

The evening was casual and Ally was wearing

sandals, a simple A-line skirt and what seemed to his untrained eye to be one tank top over another—the outer layer plain but lower cut, the other higher at the neckline so a strip of lace could peek above and entice the hell out of him.

All he knew was that she looked great with her hair falling free to her nearly bare shoulders, that he'd spent the whole workday wrangling his thoughts away from images of her to concentrate on his patients, that he'd counted the number of therapy sessions he had to get through before he could be with her again, and that even now that he was with her again, he was itching to be *alone* with her again.

But he kept that to himself. To Nina, he said only, "She's a decent person. I was wrong about her in the beginning."

"Yes, I've noticed that every time we talk you seem to have more positive things to say about her."

There was an underlying note of humor in Nina's voice and Jake recognized that it was at his expense.

"And now here you are, trying to arrange things so she moves back to Chicago," Nina added.

Jake shrugged and it made Nina laugh.

"Oh, don't act all Mr. Cool with me. You can't keep your eyes off her. You hang on every word she says. I half expect to find you drooling over her. You're worse off than you were with Claudia."

Jake tore his gaze from Ally to frown at Nina. "Should I be worried that you're hallucinating?"

"What you're worried about is Ally going back to L.A. And why would that be unless you've got it bad for her?"

"Maybe for Estelle's sake?" he theorized.

Nina laughed again. "Yeah, right," she said facetiously. "For Estelle's sake."

Jake just grinned at his friend. He wasn't fooling her, so he decided to stop trying.

"I've got it pretty bad," he confessed, thinking that if he aired out the attraction it might dissipate. Some, at least. And at the rate it was growing, anything that might cut it down to size was worth a try.

"I'm not even sure why," he confided to Nina.

"Could it be because she has big, beautiful green eyes?"

And a knock-'em-dead face and body to go with them...

"It can't be all about looks—Claudia had looks, if you'll recall."

"Ally seems nice. Caring. Sweet. Considerate."

"And buried in her job—like Claudia."

"It wasn't only that Claudia was buried in her job— if *you'll* recall," Nina reminded him. "In fact, what split up the two of you was less that than the other things."

"True."

But it remained to be seen if those *other things* proved true of Ally, too. So far it could go either way.

"And if you're worried that Ally is buried in her job," Nina said, "why are you trying to get her hired as designer for the Taka hotel chain? That's big-time work."

"But it's work she'll mainly do from here."

"Okay. So let's say we get her here. Then what's the plan?"

"No plan. Just get her here." Where the most he'd have to go without seeing her was a workday…

"Yeah, I've got it pretty bad," Jake repeated, more to himself than to his friend.

Nina moved to stand beside him where she could look at the scene on the sofa, too.

"Well, I'm all for you and Ally getting together," she announced.

"Just think," Nina added, "with Estelle and Bubby being close friends, and you and I close friends, if you and Ally and Estelle were family we could be one big happy—"

Jake cut her off by laughing wryly and playfully hooking his arm around her neck. "Don't go getting ahead of yourself, Hanson. Just because I like Ally doesn't mean I'm ready to jump in with both feet and play house the way you did."

"I did not *play* house with David," Nina protested, referring to the fact that she had been her husband's live-in assistant before they'd fallen in love and gotten married. "And I could only wish that things would work out for you and Ally the way they worked out for David and me."

"I don't know about that," Jake said.

Even as he surprised himself with a fleeting thought that that might not be so bad…

* * *

Ally glanced up from Bubby's family albums, hoping Jake and Nina might be back soon to rescue her.

But they were in the dining room, and Jake was pulling the other woman into his side with a sort of neck hug. They were smiling, laughing. The familiarity between them, the affection, was unmistakable.

There was no reason to be jealous, Ally told herself. Jake, Bubby and Nina were all close. Within minutes of meeting Nina and David Hanson it was apparent that they were a loving, devoted couple and that their family was important to them. Jake was probably merely showing Nina the kind of innocent affection a brother might show a sister.

Yet, Ally's stomach knotted up anyway.

And she put jealousy on the list of emotions this man was inspiring in her. The list that included the fact that she couldn't get him off her mind. That just knowing she was going to see him tonight had made her feel as excited as she had for her first school dance. And how she'd relived the kisses of the two previous nights at least a million times. And that she felt as obsessed as a teenager with having him kiss her again.

But odd or not, the last thing she wanted to see was him in *any* kind of clench with another woman.

He let go of Nina a moment later and they both turned to the sideboard for hors d'oeuvres.

Ally felt slightly better. But only slightly.

What exactly was between Jake and Nina Hanson? she couldn't help wondering.

They were friends—that was the party line.

But why weren't they more than that?

Nina was beautiful, sweet, kind, a little sassy.

There was no question that Jake was tremendously handsome and charismatic and interesting. And that he could kiss like no one Ally had ever kissed before.

So why hadn't they gotten together romantically? They would have made the perfect twosome. Had they always only been friends or had they been more than that at some point?

Ally didn't want to be eaten alive as much by curiosity as by jealousy, but she was. It just didn't make sense to her that these two people who seemed so right for each other, who were obviously close and cared about each other, hadn't hooked up with each other…

Or *had* they hooked up and it just hadn't worked out?

Had he ever kissed Nina the way he'd kissed her?

If he had and Nina's husband had any idea, Ally doubted Jake would be welcome in their home. So maybe they were only friends.

Not that it was any of her business. And it shouldn't have mattered to her one way or another.

But it did.

And the longer she went on looking at Jake from this distance, the less Ally could believe something more intimate hadn't existed between them. Or didn't. After all, how could Nina *not* have wanted him?

He was dressed in dark gray slacks that were almost the color of his eyes, and a dove-gray dress shirt with the sleeves rolled to his elbows. His dark hair was carelessly swept away from his sculpted face just so. He gave the impression of strength—physical strength and strength of character. When he laughed or smiled, sexy little lines gathered at the corners of his eyes.

And Ally wanted him so much it made her ache.

I have to stop this, she told herself.

It was the same thing she'd been telling herself all day. This was not the time or place to be getting involved with anyone. And he was not the man she should be getting involved with. They were just passing through each other's lives and would soon be going their separate ways, as if they'd met on a tropical vacation.

Except this *wasn't* a tropical vacation. And this didn't provide the sort of anonymity, the sort of suspension of reality, that a tropical vacation would. This was the kind of situation where feelings could be bruised. Where grudges could be held. Where the future of her mother's friendships could be damaged.

And I could get hurt.

Because she liked Jake Fox too much, she finally admitted. And every moment she spent with him, every look they shared, every touch, every kiss, only made her like him more.

But it didn't change the fact that when everything was settled with her mother, they would both go on with their separate lives. She'd be left hearing about him through her mother—what he was doing, who he was seeing, who he was involved with.

And as bad as she ached for him, Ally knew it would be so much worse to get in any deeper with Jake now, and then be a distant, removed observer of his life evolving without her.

So much worse that it made her feel awful just imagining it.

Awful enough to convince her that she really, really needed to leave last night's kiss finally behind her and not repeat it.

Because that was the only solution she could come up with to keep this from going any further than it already had.

Chapter Ten

As Jake had driven Ally and Estelle home, Ally had been determined that she would say good-night and not end up alone with him again.

But as they'd pulled into the driveway, Estelle had announced that she was going straight to bed, asking Jake if she would see him the following morning for their walk. Jake had promised that she would and complained that he'd missed Monday morning's excursion. Estelle had suggested that he and Ally make up for that by taking a walk right then. And since Estelle's behavior was increasingly less erratic now that she was taking her medication and she could be trusted to stay safely in her bed once she got there, Ally hadn't had much of an excuse.

Which was how she had ended up alone with Jake after all.

"Have you made any decisions about Estelle's living arrangements?" he asked as they headed for the neighborhood park.

"No," Ally admitted. "And I need to. I need to get back to L.A., to work. Trying to get things done long-distance is a pain. I was on the phone a dozen times today and did what I could on my laptop, but decorating is a visual thing—even though my assistant sent me scans of fabric samples, it isn't the same as seeing the actual sample. I didn't dare make my choices that way, and work is piling up."

"But that didn't convince you to do anything about the housing stuff?"

"I thought about it—" When she hadn't been thinking about him. "I even tried to hint at it with Mother."

"How did you do that?"

"I pointed out the downside of home ownership, asked if she ever thought of living in an apartment."

"And?"

"She thought I was talking about taking her with me to California again and even on her thyroid medicine she bit my head off. After that I didn't have the courage to bring up assisted living. Especially when I didn't feel as if I could say anything really great about it, knowing what she'd have to give up to move."

They reached the well-lit park and began to stroll along the path that circled it.

Assisted living was an upsetting topic for Ally and she didn't want to talk more about it. So she decided instead to use their walk to find out more about his friendship with Nina.

"So," she said. "Nina. I like her."

"She likes you, too. She told me before dinner, when you were stuck looking at Bubby's photographs."

There was laughter in his voice and Ally knew he'd found it funny that she'd been trapped for so long with family albums of people she didn't even know.

"Yeah, thanks for that," Ally said, laughing. "I kept waiting to be saved and all the two of you did was stay away so you didn't have to look at the pictures."

"Guilty as charged," he confessed. "But in our defense, we've both seen them a trillion times."

"I saw you and Nina in the dining room," Ally said then. "Are you sure you're just friends?" she added in a teasing tone.

"Yep, just friends."

"How long have you known each other?"

"We met working our first jobs in a grocery store as teenagers. We've been friends ever since."

"But even then you didn't date or like each other as more than that?"

"Nope."

"How come? Does Nina know something about you that I should know?"

He laughed. "What is all this about, Ally?"

"I was just thinking—watching the two of you in the

dining room—that you would make an ideal couple. And yet you're not together…"

"Is that what you were thinking?" he said, sounding as if he knew better.

"You don't agree?"

He shrugged. "I guess that depends on what *ideal* means."

"You look good together. You seem to have similar tastes and senses of humor and—"

"Except for the looking-good-together part, isn't the rest of that what causes people to be friends?"

Ally sighed. He was enjoying making this difficult.

Jake ran a hand through his hair. "Look, when I met Nina I had a lot to contend with—it was my first week in a group home, I was on probation, I wasn't sure if I was going to get to finish high school or if I was going to have to get a G.E.D., I was having court-mandated therapy—basically I'd screwed up royally and was paying the price for it. Girls weren't an option for me. But I was working side by side with Nina, we'd talk, and we became friends."

"She didn't want to be more than that either?"

Jake nudged her with his shoulder. "Can't believe it, huh?"

Ally had to smile at his egotism. "Only asking," she demurred.

"I *was* quite a catch with my police record, bad skin, and clothes that had come from the freebie bin at Social Services. But Nina was dating someone else—the guy she ended up marrying and having two kids with by the time she was twenty-two. We were both on our own separate rocky paths. What we offered each other was that unconditional support that teenagers give other teenagers, and that's just how it's always been with us."

"And you never—"

"Never," he said definitively. "I love her like a sister. I think she'd say she loves me like a brother. In a lot of ways, Nina—and Bubby by association—are the only family I've ever known."

As they passed the halfway point on the path, Ally's curiosity only grew.

"So if not Nina, why not someone else?" she asked.

"As a teenager? I told you—"

"No, not as a teenager. You are old enough to have moved on to adult relationships, you know. Have you ever been married?"

"Never."

"Hmm," Ally mused. "I would have thought that marrying and making a family of your own would have been a goal."

He shrugged. "It's not something I'm willing to do just for the sake of doing it. I want a family, but I sure as hell don't want a marriage that doesn't work out and leaves me losing the family I start."

That was a good point.

"Have you ever gotten close to marrying?" Ally persisted.

"Recently, as a matter of fact. A little over a year ago."

"Really…"

"Really. I was engaged to a woman named Claudia. She was an investment banker."

"Why didn't it work out between you?"

"Looking for more flaws in me?" he joked.

Looking for *any* flaws in him was more like it.

"Yes," she confessed, but in a tone that made it sound as if she was teasing him.

"Sorry, but it was me who opted out, not her. We just reached a point where I realized that while she seemed perfect for me in most ways, I couldn't handle her view of family."

"She didn't want one?"

"It wasn't that. We talked about having kids—she saw that for herself. But it was the way she treated the family she already had that got to me."

"Did she already *have* kids?"

"No. I mean her parents, her sister, her aunt. I believed her when she said she wanted to spend more time with them but was just too busy with work, with me."

"Only that wasn't the case?"

"She was busy," he allowed. "But she also didn't really want to be bothered with her family. They all lived nearby, but they might as well have been in another country. Her only contact with them most of the time was through periodic phone calls that she complained about having to make. But I was still buying the busy-excuse until she found out her dad was dying."

"What happened then?" Ally asked.

"Dying or not, Claudia wasn't going to alter her own routine or let it interrupt her life. Her dad was in hospice for two weeks and she saw him three times—all three of those times I had to make her go or she wouldn't have gone even then."

"Maybe it was just too hard for her emotionally. Maybe keeping her distance was how she protected herself."

"Who was it easy for? For her mother or her sister or her aunt who were having to deal with everything while Claudia went on about her business? That isn't easy for anybody and no one gets a free pass just because it's hard. But with Claudia it wasn't even that. She didn't want to get her hands dirty. Even the day we got word that her father was hours away from dying, I met her at the hospice, she stayed a few minutes and then said there was nothing she could do anyway, she was going back to work. *I* ended up staying with her family until her dad passed—with instructions from her to call and let her know when it was over. That was when I decided she wasn't for me."

"So you broke it off."

"Not at the funeral or anything. But soon after that. Then I cried on Nina's shoulder just like she'd cried on mine when her first marriage broke up. Because we're *friends,*" he said, goading Ally a little.

They'd come full circle on the park path, so they crossed the street to go home.

"Okay, I get it," Ally said with a show of exasperation, "you and Nina are *just friends.*"

"But it's so much fun that you're jealous."

"In your dreams, Dr. Fox," she said. Convincingly, she thought.

They'd reached her house and went around to the backyard. They were climbing the stairs to her apartment when he put an arm around her shoulders and pulled her to his side in a much more suggestive way than the headlock she'd witnessed him putting on Nina.

"You *are* in my dreams," he said into her ear.

"Liar," she accused as they stepped onto the landing. She unlocked the door and opened it, flipping on the light inside. But she didn't make any move to go in.

"Absolute truth," he swore. "You've taken over my conscious and my unconscious."

It was very satisfying to have his arm around her in a way that wasn't merely playful and to hear that she was on his mind as much as he was on hers. Maybe too satisfying, because she lost her grip on some of that earlier determination to keep him at bay and turned in the circle of his arm to face him.

"That sounds very distracting," she said as if she could hardly imagine it.

"Very," he agreed with a sexy smile.

She tipped her chin upward, meeting his charcoal-colored eyes with hers, basking in the heat of his gaze as his mouth met hers.

Ally felt Jake's arms twine around her and every thought of refusing him evaporated as lips parted and that kiss went from sweet to sensual just that quick.

His mouth opened wider and his tongue came to meet hers. Ally wasn't shy, either, not when she was so glad to be back in his arms.

Jake pulled her close with a hand flat to her back, his fingers a gentle but firm undulation there that lured her another step away from reason.

Heat crept through her body as she reacted to his touch, and she tried to ignore it, but with every inching of that kiss into more intimate territory, every press of his fingers into her back, her body just seemed to scream for attention.

Her hand slinked its way under his shirtsleeve. And while there was nothing overtly seductive about it, it somehow seemed a little forbidden.

Maybe to Jake, too, because it prompted him to pull her closer still, enough for her breasts to come up against his chest.

Not that that calmed what her body was crying out for. It didn't. Somehow she thought he could sense that because his kiss became even deeper, even more hungry, even more intense.

He kept her clasped tight to his body as he spun them both into the open door and around so that Ally was pinned between him and the wall. That hand at her waist slipped under the hem of her shirt, leaving nothing between her body and that big, strong, adept hand coursing slowly, slowly up to breasts that were nearly heaving with need.

Then he reached one straining globe and her breath

caught in her throat at that first touch that sent a chill of delight quivering through her.

Her shoulders drew back and her spine arched. And the meeting of their mouths became hardly a kiss at all but something more raw, more sexual, to accompany that hand that was kneading her flesh, encasing her, encompassing her, gently tugging her nipple, teasing it, twirling fingertips around it, and altogether turning her to mush inside.

He was up against her, the length of his body running the length of hers, and Ally hated every thread of the clothing that came between them.

She tore his shirttails from his waistband and plunged both of her arms underneath with such vigor she was surprised that the buttons didn't fly. Not that she would have cared if they had. All she cared about was laying her palms to the breadth of his bare back.

The bed was only a few feet away—that thought came as a yearning for even more began to stir in her.

She could click off the light.

She could reach over and close the door.

But you weren't even supposed to kiss him tonight.

Why she remembered that at that moment she didn't know. But once she had, it wouldn't let her ignore it.

There were reasons she'd come to that conclusion, she told herself. And if she shouldn't even kiss him, she *definitely* shouldn't be doing anything else.

Ally slowly pulled her arms out from under Jake's shirt and pushed slightly away from him.

"I wasn't even supposed to kiss you tonight," she told him when she'd broken off the kiss, too, saying out loud what had been going through her head for the last few minutes.

"Why not?" he asked, nibbling the side of her neck and more firmly caressing her breast.

Firmly enough to make her less inclined to stop this at all...

"I'm not sure," she answered, "but I told myself not to." Reluctantly he let go, taking his hand out from under her shirts, putting it back on her waist.

"Okay. Whatever you say," he conceded amiably. Then he placed a soft kiss to the top of her ear and whispered, "But you know, not everything I do has a geriatric twist to it."

Ally laughed. "I didn't think it did."

"I just wanted you to have the information. In case."

"Good to know," she said, playing along and appreciating that he was making light of this so it wasn't awkward.

He kissed her again, his lips parted but his tongue keeping a respectful distance. And still it was enough to send her blood rushing through her veins to chip away at her determination.

But then he stepped back into the doorway to tuck in his shirt and lean against the jamb.

"So, tomorrow night—the Senior Follies?" he said.

"That's my understanding," Ally confirmed their plans to attend a potluck dinner and some sort of variety show at the senior center.

She turned to mirror his stance, leaning a shoulder to the wall she'd been up against a moment before. But she couldn't merely let her arms dangle at her sides the way his were, she had to cross hers over the front of her because she knew her nipples were still making their presence known and poking visibly through the thin knit of her shirts.

Jake reached over and brushed a strand of hair from her face, letting his palm rest on her cheek for a moment afterward, his eyes looking deeply into hers before he pulled his hand away again.

"Till then?" he said.

Did he know she still wanted him enough to reconsider her decision?

But she stuck to it. With difficulty.

"Till then," she said, proud of the strength she managed to put into it.

He smiled a half smile, as if he knew better anyway, but he didn't comment on it. Instead, he said, "Okay, but don't spend tomorrow making rules I'm just gonna have to break."

Ally couldn't help laughing again.

"Maybe I won't let you break any more of them," she challenged his cockiness.

But he just grinned. A big, broad, knowing grin.

Then he said a simple good-night, pushed off the doorjamb and disappeared down the stairs.

Chapter Eleven

Tuesday evening at the Wilkens Senior Center was an eye-opening experience for Ally. For no particular reason, she'd expected that the potluck dinner and Senior Follies would be a sedate gathering of a few elderly people who would sit slumped in chairs like aged wallflowers, exchanging laments about physical ailments before falling asleep to more oldsters singing choir-type music.

Instead, to her surprise, the community center was packed with seniors and their friends and family all mingling and chatting happily.

The meal itself—which was the first portion of the event—was heavy with tuna-noodle casseroles and didn't thrill either Ally or Jake, but the entire dinner hour was so upbeat that Ally didn't mind eating very little. And the only complaint from anyone was that government regulations wouldn't allow them to serve liquor on the premises.

By the time everyone filed into the larger, gymnasiumlike room where folding chairs were lined up in rows facing a makeshift stage, Ally abandoned the idea that the audience would sleep through any portion of what was to come, and wondered what that might be.

Nina had to be at a function for one of her children, so Bubby had come with Ally, Estelle and Jake. Once Ally and Jake were seated, Estelle and Bubby left them to go behind the scenes.

Ally had already seen a change come over her mother when they'd first arrived at the center. Estelle was full of life, greeting everyone effusively, joking with them, even flirting slightly with a few of the older men. When Estelle left to go backstage with Bubby, Ally assumed they were helping with costumes or some other details and was just impressed that her mother was participating at all.

The show the audience was treated to was more professional than anything Ally had imagined. Singing was definitely the predominant entertainment—by duos, trios and a barbershop quartet—but not a single sour note was to be heard, and rather than choir music, some of the songs were slightly bawdy.

There was a dramatic reading that bordered on mind-numbingly dull, but the ventriloquist act was well done and funny, and the two comedy routines were both ribald.

And then the final performance was announced and out came Bubby, Estelle and three of their other walking companions.

They were dressed in loose-fitting, sequined jump-suits, they had bright red feather boas draped over their shoulders, and fishnet stockings peeked from below their hems and above the tap shoes they were all wearing.

"Mother?" Ally muttered in shock just before the fivesome proceeded to do a hilarious dance that was saucy and outrageous and included everything from tap to a mimicry of a striptease that sent the boas out into the crowd.

When they linked arms and added a touch of the Rockettes, Ally said to Jake, "Can my mother do that?" thinking about the recent fall that still had Estelle's wrist in a brace.

"Looks like she can. I think they're all holding each other up," he answered, proceeding to add a wolf whistle to the hoots and hollers that the rest of the onlookers were doing to cheer them on.

Altogether, the dance was campy and over the top and, when it was finished, it was met with a standing ovation and rousing applause that made it the most popular of the acts.

The chorus line accepted their adoration with a bow— arms still linked, the five ladies bent forward at the waist—and stayed humbly head-lowered for at least thirty seconds. Then they straightened up, broke into gales of laughter themselves, hugging each other and proving no one had enjoyed their dance more than they had.

And from her position in the midst of the audience, Ally just looked on in amazement.

"Who *was* that woman and what did she do with Estelle Rogers?" Ally said to Jake when they were finally alone later that evening.

Her mother's exuberance had lasted the remainder of the night—even offstage as Estelle, Bubby and their other friends accepted praise for their performance, and Estelle had been humming on her way to bed after bidding Ally and Jake good-night when they'd arrived home from dropping Bubby off at her apartment.

That was when Jake had confided that he was starving, Ally had said she was, too, and he'd used his cell phone to place an order for Chinese food to be delivered. They were sitting on the front porch waiting for it.

"I thought your jaw was going to hit the floor when you saw your mother come out onto that stage tonight," he said, laughing.

"Did you know she was going to dance?"

"Sure. It's been a hot topic of discussion on our walks. But with the way your mother has been declining, everyone was afraid she wouldn't be up to it. They were thrilled when she said she was feeling so much better that she thought she could go through with the performance. I guess she didn't tell you, though."

"No, she didn't," Ally said. "And if I hadn't seen it with my own eyes I wouldn't have believed it."

"I had that impression," he said with a chuckle.

The heat of the night air would have been stifling if not for the breeze that wafted around them. And besides the cooling effects, it also brought the scent of Jake's cologne—something Ally liked as much as the smell of the flowers that grew just below the porch.

He'd said he'd had time to go home before they were due at the senior center, and Ally thought that he'd shaved and changed out of his work clothes because he had on a rust-colored sport shirt with brown twill slacks that didn't have a wrinkle in them. Once again his sleeves were rolled to his elbows, which made it difficult for Ally not to think about the way she'd run her hand up his forearm and underneath his sleeve the night before. Even more difficult for her not to want to do it again.

"Didn't you approve?" he asked her, drawing her back into their conversation.

"Of the dance? Oh, no, it isn't that. I just…my mother was like a different person tonight."

"She seemed like the same person to me."

"That's the Estelle Rogers *you* know—is that what you're telling me?"

"Well, she isn't out doing mock stripteases every day, no. But this is a side of her I know, sure."

"It isn't a side of her I know."

Jake had been such a complete gentleman all evening that there hadn't been any indication of what they'd shared the previous night and it occurred to Ally then that everyone had sides of themselves they could hide at will.

Or maybe he had decided that he wasn't going to pursue whatever it was that kept cropping up between them.

Which should have made Ally happy.

And yet that possibility didn't please her at all.

"I've never seen my mother like that," she said, attempting to keep to the subject and ignore her wandering thoughts. "She wasn't even that fun-loving or carefree or…I don't know—girlish, I guess…before my dad died. But tonight…" Ally shook her head. "Really, she was like a different person."

Jake leaned close enough to nudge her with his shoulder and whisper, "But fun—like the other night with the margaritas. That's one of the reasons I like her—you never know when she might cut loose."

"So this is your Estelle—someone who cuts loose?" Ally said.

"You should see her on poker night, but, yeah, that's all part of *my* Estelle," he confirmed. "Not that I haven't seen the leathery side of her, too, but—"

"The leathery side of her is usually *all* I get."

"Not tonight," he pointed out.

And Ally had to concede that he was right. Tonight, at the senior center, Estelle hadn't been her usual leathery self with Ally either. Which had only added to Ally's amazement.

"Maybe you could look at it this way," Jake suggested. "When Estelle was raising you, she needed to be the parent to your child. A parent needs to set the limits, enforce the boundaries, and so on. And the child needs to be the child—to test the limits, to step over the boundaries, to get out of line sometimes. Parent and child aren't supposed to be friends—other people fill those roles for them. But at this stage of your lives, you both have the chance to put that aside and get to know each other in a different way. And maybe become friends."

Ally wasn't sure if that was possible. But rather than say that to Jake she said, "Tonight just made it all the more clear that Mother has really sort of found her niche with Bubby and the rest of her friends, and at the senior center."

Jake shrugged. "I haven't seen any signs that she's unhappy, that's for sure. She just can't do everything on her own anymore and that frustrates her and probably scares and worries her—although of course she would never admit it. But that's Estelle. Like I've said— enough times before that you're probably sick of hearing it—she just needs some help now."

"But what if the help does more harm than good?"

"You're still worrying about moving her away from all this," Jake surmised.

"More now, after tonight, after seeing for myself what a good time she's having." Ally sighed. "Now the decisions I have to make are so much harder."

Jake put his arm around her, pulling her to his side. "Maybe a new solution will present itself," he said.

Ally turned her head to look at him again, never tiring of the sight of that handsome face.

"Yeah, right," she said dubiously. "Because new solutions present themselves all the time."

"You never know…"

A car with the name of a Chinese restaurant pulled up to the curb just then and to Ally's disappointment, Jake pulled away to go get the food.

Leaving her with the rear view of him.

And thoughts that had nothing whatsoever to do with her mother.

Chapter Twelve

With sacks of Chinese food in hand, Ally and Jake went around the house to her apartment.

Ally had gone up soon after they'd arrived home to turn on her fans and open her windows to air the place out. Not because she'd planned on having company—or so she'd told herself—but for the sake of her own comfort when she went to bed later.

While she was up there she'd also paused long enough to run a brush through her hair and apply a little lip gloss. She was wearing a simple, snug-fitting black knit dress cut in at a sharp angle at the shoulders, and a pair of sandals. But because the sandals hurt, when she and Jake reached the now-cooler apartment, she kicked them off, leaving her feet bare.

"Let's skip dishes and just eat out of the cartons," Jake suggested.

Ally agreed, so, sitting on the sofa, they shared the food, laughing again over incidents and jokes from the Senior Follies.

Then they disposed of the food containers and without discussion returned to the sofa. One of Jake's arms was stretched across the top of the back cushions, Ally's legs were tucked under her left hip, and despite knowing she shouldn't be settling in so cozily with him, it was too nice for her to do anything to disturb it.

"Now tell me about the other side of Ally," Jake said as they both popped peppermints from the candy dish Ally had on the coffee table.

"You already know about the daughter side," she said. "And about the work side—"

"What about the personal side?" he qualified, like so many other times, seeming to know her train of thought.

"Ah," she said. "Well, I'm single—but you know that, too. And beyond that, I work so much there isn't a lot of time for a personal side."

"Come on, look at you—there have to be men all over the place who want you. What am I up against?"

She'd like it if he were up against her—that was what flashed through her mind. But she certainly didn't say it. And she tried not to think anymore about it either. Or to be too delighted that he was trying to find out if he had any competition.

"If there are men all over the place who want me they're keeping it pretty quiet," she said, opting for honesty over coyness.

Jake smiled as if she was being coy anyway. "You're telling me there's no one and never has been? That you've been the cloistered designer since leaving Chicago? In L.A. of all places?"

"I have not been the cloistered designer—I didn't say that. But you didn't ask if there has ever been anyone."

"So there *was* someone, at some point," he said as if he'd hammered it out of her. "Were you married?"

"No, I've never been married. But, like you, I was engaged once and we lived together."

"Engaged to…"

"Sean Coffman. We met four years ago, when he was a contractor on a house I was designing interiors for."

"Work, work, work—that's the thread that runs through everything with you, isn't it?"

Ally shrugged and took his observation lightly because it was delivered along with a stroke of his palm to the back of her head.

"Is Sean Coffman the only time you set your sights on the altar?" Jake asked then.

"Yes," Ally answered, her voice a tiny bit breathy because even an innocent caress from him did that to her.

"And how come you didn't get there?"

"To the altar? I broke it off. For the opposite reason

you ended your relationship with Claudia." Ally hated thinking about him with anyone else and couldn't bring herself to say the woman's name without a hint of a derogatory inflection.

"You've lost me," Jake said. "What's the opposite reason?"

"You broke up with Claudia because she wasn't close enough to her family."

"Actually it was more the kind of person she was in regards to her family."

"Well, Sean had too much family. He was one of nine kids. His father had seven siblings, his mother had ten. Sean was the oldest of forty-six cousins—"

"That would make for big holiday dinners."

"Which probably appeals to you," Ally guessed.

Jake shrugged. "The more the merrier."

Ally shook her head and rolled her eyes.

"So let me get this straight," Jake said. "You dumped the guy because he came from a big family?"

Ally could tell by Jake's frown that he disapproved.

"No, I did not *dump* him because he came from a big family. I ended the engagement because he couldn't separate himself from that big family."

More of the frown greeted that.

"Here's how it was," Ally explained. "Sean and I met, dated—alone most of the time—and then he asked me to move in with him. But once I did that, everything changed and I started having to live the way Sean lived."

"Which meant?"

"Which meant that I can't even tell you how many people had keys to our apartment. Every time I turned around there was a cousin or a brother or a sister there— crashing because their own place was being painted or fumigated or whatever, raiding the fridge, watching our TV because theirs was broken, using our washer and dryer, chilling out because they'd had a fight with a parent or a girlfriend or a spouse—"

"I get the idea."

"And it wasn't only the apartment. If we were going out to dinner or a movie or shopping, it had to be with an entourage of family. He didn't even propose to me by himself!"

"He did it in a group?"

"He'd sworn that we were going to have a night out alone. I was supposed to meet him at a bar for a drink and from there we would have every minute to ourselves. He said he wouldn't even answer the cell phone that rang constantly with family members' calls. But when I got to the bar not only weren't we alone, he'd rented the place out so there wasn't anyone in it *but* his family—four grandparents and all. And a bunch of them were holding up a banner that said, Will You Marry Sean, while Sean was on one knee in front of them all with a ring."

Jake flinched and laughed at once. "Hard to say no to that."

"And it wasn't that I wanted to say no. Sean was a good guy and I loved him—that was why I said yes to the group proposal. And I liked his family, too—most of them anyway. So I said yes, but after the party I told him that things had to be different, that we had to limit the amount of time with his family and concentrate on just the two of us."

"Did he accept that?"

"He said he did."

"But…"

Ally shook her head again. "It just didn't happen. Sean liked always having his relatives around. That more-the-merrier thing? I don't think a day went by when he didn't say that. The only thing that was different after the engagement was that he got sneakier about how he included his family in everything we did. And they were always there—just happening to drop in when we were having movie night, coincidentally at the same restaurant, the same theater, the same mall—"

"So you figured he was still getting the word out, he was just doing it behind your back."

"It was obvious, yes."

"And all that family togetherness—"

"Drove me crazy."

"Too much of a good thing."

"Way, way too much," Ally confirmed.

"So you called off the wedding," Jake concluded.

"I kept trying not to have to." Ally couldn't keep the sadness from creeping into her tone. "I did everything I could think of to have some alone-time with Sean, to make him understand that I needed that. That having his family around every minute made me feel like I wasn't enough for him."

She hadn't meant for her voice to crack. It certainly hadn't been a ploy to get Jake to curve his hand around her neck—although once it was there it was firm and reassuring, and she wasn't going to reject it…

"Anyway, I wanted what my parents had had—to be part of a couple that was so into each other that almost nothing could penetrate it. But Sean wanted things the way they were and I finally had to accept that that was just what life with him was—if you were with Sean, you were with all the Coffmans. And I couldn't do it."

"Sounds like that was the smartest move. As much as I've always envied family—especially big ones—I think that would have driven me crazy, too." Jake traced her hairline from her temple to a spot behind her ear that she'd never known could be so sensitive. "And was that your only near miss with marriage?" he asked.

"You only had one, but you think I should have had more?" she challenged.

He smiled slyly. "Like I said, look at you…"

He was, too. With those dark eyes that glistened with a kind of single-minded attention that Sean had never shown her.

Maybe that was why she was so susceptible to this man.

Maybe that and the fact that it *had* been three years since she'd been with anyone else.

But even as that thought went through her mind, Ally

knew it wasn't three years of loneliness influencing her. This attraction was all about Jake.

"I think maybe that guy just didn't know what he was missing," he said then, doing another slow massage of her nape, this one more seductive than comforting. "I know I like being alone with you so much that it's all I can think about..." Jake smiled a wicked smile. "Well, not *all* I can think about about you, but it's definitely a part of the package."

His hand went up to the back of her head again, supporting it as he leaned forward and kissed her.

She just liked that too much, she told herself when it seemed as if it was what she'd been waiting for since she'd sent him home the night before.

The kiss was short, though, before he ended it and looked into her eyes again.

"Did you make rules I need to break tonight?" he asked, referring to what she'd told him about having forbidden herself this same thing last night.

"No new ones," she said with a small smile.

He kissed her again, slightly longer, slightly slower.

"What about those reasons you couldn't remember? Did you remember them?"

The reasons she hadn't been able to recall for *why* she'd forbidden herself these kisses.

"I believe it had something to do with complicating things."

"Too ambiguous to be a good reason not to do anything," he judged before kissing her again.

"And there was something about this not being a tropical vacation..." she added in the brief space between kisses.

"How would it be different if it was?"

"Oh, you know...vacation flings..."

"I want more than that," he said. But he said it just before the next kiss brought with it his tongue to give a languid invitation to hers and take her a step further away from rational thought.

Maybe if Sean had kissed her like that she *would* have married him in spite of his family.

There was just something so adept in Jake's every movement, every nuance...

And Ally wanted things, too. She wanted *him.* She wanted everything he could do for her. And she was tired of fighting it. Somewhere along the way, Jake had become an oasis for her. He soothed her, made her feel things that were so much better.

And that was what she wanted tonight. To step completely into the oasis. To leave everything else behind and give in to all that was just between the two of them. Without worrying about any consequences.

He pulled away and once more looked into her eyes, his own intense and glistening with a desire Ally recognized because it was alive in her, too.

"Break them, bend them or abide by them?" he asked, his voice rich and husky with emotion.

"My rules?"

"Your rules."

Ally gave herself one final opportunity to say no to him, but she just couldn't deny herself tonight. Not when she couldn't think of anything that mattered as much as she wanted him.

"Throw them out the window," she suggested, craning upward enough to kiss him this time.

She felt him smile as his lips parted. Kissing him now was raucous, rowdy, unruly—mouths were opened wide and his tongue was devilishly rambunctious, demanding the same of hers until everything became a blur to Ally and her senses took over.

His hands were in her hair, bracketing her face, caressing her neck, squeezing her shoulders. He smelled of that clean, heady cologne, he tasted of mint, and he exuded a sexual heat that seemed to infuse her and ignite the same thing in her.

Somewhere along the way her own hands had come to be on his chest and they seemed to move of their own volition to the buttons of his shirt, unfastening them, yanking the tails free of his pants and then meandering inside to his naked chest.

Perfect pectorals met her, male nibs tightening in response to her touch, but no comparison for the taut, crowning crests of her own breasts as they yearned for the same attention.

Ally coursed her way up and over his broad shoulders, taking with her the shirt she finagled off his arms and cast aside.

The feel of her skin against his only inspired the need in her for more of it. She reached behind her to the zipper that held her dress closed and again felt Jake's grin as he took her hands away and did the honors himself.

But at a pace that was so slow it was agony for Ally, who could only deal with that anguish by letting her palms stroke his well-honed biceps, his pecs and shoulders, his broad back...

But then, as if something occurred to him, he stopped it all and leaned away from her. Pointing a thumb to the switch on the wall next to the door, he said, "Lights or no lights?"

Ally feasted on the sight of him—flat, well-defined abdominals; the ever-widening V of a torso that would have made an underwear model's fortune; those tremendous shoulders and arms—and being able to go on seeing him was a distinct positive.

But her dress was about to come off. And he'd be able to see her just as openly as she was ogling him...

An instant of inhibition made her say, "Off."

Jake stood and went to the switch. He flipped it off, but the small apartment didn't go completely black—there was a full moon tonight and its creamy glow flooded in through windows whose curtains were open.

It was in that light that Jake came to the couch again. Standing tall beside it, he held out a hand to her.

Ally took it, getting to her feet at his urging.

Keeping her hand, he led her to the bed, swinging her around to face him once they were there.

And that was when he sent her dress to the floor, leaving her in nothing but her strapless bra and panties.

He had to look—she could tell he couldn't resist, and she was glad she'd opted to have only moonglow illuminating his scrutiny. He devoured her with his eyes, the groan that rumbled from his throat showing approval for the sexy black lace thong and the matching bra that held her bulging from its top.

And okay, yes, maybe the chance that he would see her in it *had* been a fleeting thought when she'd gotten dressed, but she certainly didn't regret it now. Especially not when Jake leaned down and kissed the swells of each breast from above the cups, obviously relishing what he was seeing before he unhooked the bra, letting it fall away.

This time Jake didn't stare, though. After an appreciative glance he kissed her again, his mouth, his tongue playful, while he took something from his pocket and tossed it to the mattress. Then he rid himself of the rest of his own clothes and Ally of her panties, too.

Mouths parted so he could gently ease her onto the bed and Ally was treated to a brief glimpse of the rest of him—an athlete's legs, narrow hips and long, hard proof of his intentions. He was a spectacular specimen of masculinity, a design she couldn't have improved upon, and she was only too glad to have him join her on the bed.

Lying on his side, his big body running the length of hers, he kissed her once more, his left arm bracing his weight while his right hand rested on her hip. His thumb was doing feathery strokes that tickled slightly and enticed deliciously just before that hand began a leisurely journey up to her waist.

Again, more leisurely than Ally would have liked when her breasts were aching for his attention, her nipples tight little knots of yearning, and the hunger for him churning inside of her.

His hand went from her waist to her rib cage, doing that tantalizing massage there until Ally's shoulders drew back involuntarily in answer to the ever-increasing demands of her body.

She felt the smile and knew he was tormenting her on purpose, but his hand finally reached her breast, taking it into a firm but tender grip and letting her nipple tighten all the more into his palm.

She'd wondered today if she was remembering his touch to be better than it actually had been, if her memory had glorified it. But, no, it felt every bit as good as she'd recalled—and longed to feel again. Better even.

Kneading, pressing, manipulating her flesh, he had talents he hadn't even displayed the night before, spending just the right amount of time caressing her, just the right amount teasing and tempting, and toying with her nipple until a frenzy of need was born in her.

Ally's own hands went roaming over his body. She drew them up his back, around his shoulders, down his oh-so-flat belly and lower still, finding that impressive shaft she'd barely had the chance to see.

Jake moaned and for a while it was Ally who did the tormenting, the teasing, the controlling of how much pleasure she bestowed and how much she withheld, until she could tell she'd erupted the same burning needs in him that were flaming in her.

He stole a moment to sheathe himself before he refocused on her, taking her breast into his mouth.

His tongue flitted across the very tip of her nipple, flicking, fluttering, as his hand slipped between her legs.

Lost in her own delights, Ally had loosened her grip on him, but she tightened it now, sliding up, sliding down, again driving him as wild as he was driving her with fingers that found their way inside of her.

Ally's hips arched away from the mattress, moving her closer to Jake.

He caught her with the hand that had been otherwise occupied a split second before, splaying it against her rear to bring her more completely to her side. Then he raised her leg to drape over his own hip.

She let go of him as he carefully slipped into her, fitting his body to hers as if he were the missing piece.

His mouth had abandoned her breast but it didn't matter then, not when he was filling her, moving into and out of her, holding her in precisely the right position, each slow, measured penetration, each scant withdrawal building new heights of passion, of craving, of need.

Ally clung to him, moved with him, against him, holding on as tightly to him as he was holding on to her, striving for that pinnacle that each movement brought her closer to.

And then there it was—wave after wave of ecstasy that wiped away awareness of anything else, of everything else. It held her in its grip, suspended her breathing, her thought process, and set her adrift in a sea of bright colors and bliss more powerful than anything she'd ever known before.

As powerful as what appeared to overtake Jake just as she began her descent from that exquisite crescendo. Because that was when he plunged even more deeply into her, melding his body with hers while he stiffened, arched and froze at a peak that seemed to equal hers.

Then he came back to himself, too, relaxing each tensed muscle one at a time, loosening his hold on Ally enough for her to relax as well, as they both caught their breath and deflated into replete exhaustion.

For a time neither of them said anything. Jake's face was in her hair, Ally's forehead was against the wall of his chest, and all they did was bask in that moment they'd just shared.

Only when she could summon the energy, did Ally say, "Nope, nothing geriatric about *that*."

Jake laughed a low, throaty laugh. "I told you," he bragged.

He kissed the top of her head again, then drew away enough to reach her mouth with his in a kiss that was raw and purely primal.

When it ended they both collapsed again, arms and

legs entwined, face-to-face now, Jake's hands rubbing her back.

"How do you think Estelle would feel about finding me here in the morning?" he asked then.

"I think she might have a gun," Ally joked.

"That bad, huh?"

But even though it might be tempting fate, the thought of him getting up and leaving right then was not one she wanted to entertain.

So she said, "On the other hand…" and drew one of hers up his naked side, under the arm he still had around her. "Mother's alarm is right next to the intercom I bought that first day. The alarm blasts through here loud enough to wake the dead, then she snoozes for half an hour before it goes off again and she gets up…"

"I forgot that you have to listen for her—she can't hear what goes on on this end, though, can she?"

Ally smiled at the concern in his tone. "No, I have that part turned off," she assured.

He smiled with satisfaction then. "So if I leave at the first alarm—"

"You could sneak away before she knows you were here all night."

"Does that mean I can stay?" he asked, his massage of her back becoming more arousing than it had been a moment earlier.

"I think that's what it means."

"Good. Because I have plans…"

"Dinner and dancing?"

He kissed a kiss of promise then settled his head on his arm and grinned at her. "The second course of this meal, maybe. And if you want to do a dance for me…"

Ally laughed. "There are no poles in here. Besides, don't you need a little breather?"

"The second course *would* be more impressive after a recoup nap."

"Then by all means—nap," she encouraged.

He smiled again, a drowsier smile as his eyes closed.

Ally let her own drift shut, settling in against him and hoping that they both didn't fall so deeply asleep that not only didn't they wake for another round of lovemaking, but that they slept through Estelle's alarm, too.

But it was a risk Ally was willing to take.

Because whether or not they made love again, at that moment there was nothing she wanted as much as to stay right where she was.

In Jake's arms.

Chapter Thirteen

Jake and Ally had already been awake when the sound of Estelle's first alarm had come over the intercom Wednesday morning. They'd just made love for the third time and Jake had been in Ally's bed, holding her, waiting for that signal that he would have to leave. Dreading it.

So when it had come he'd been able to get out of there before Estelle knew he'd spent the night.

He'd been able to, but he hadn't wanted to.

Three hours later, as he stood at the framed window in his office nursing a cup of coffee, he was still thinking about Ally. And just how much he'd hated leaving her this morning.

He'd hated it like crazy.

He'd had his share of relationships along the way, and of course there had been Claudia. But never had there been what he'd found with Ally.

He would have never guessed that this could happen to him. Not so fast. Not with this woman, who only a week ago he'd believed was just another Claudia when it came to her family, just another Claudia who he couldn't respect and certainly wouldn't want in his life.

But now?

Now having Ally in his life was all he could think about.

It was what he was thinking about when he should have been preparing for his next group.

But he just couldn't help it.

"Physician, heal thyself," he said wryly to his reflection.

Only he didn't want help or healing. He wanted Ally.

And, no, she was not just another Claudia. Not by a long shot.

Sure, she was career driven, distant from her mother, focused on her own ambitions and life.

But he'd been allowed to look beneath the surface and understand that Ally had endured a situation that was hardly warm and fuzzy. It was no wonder Ally had gotten as far from that as possible and set her sights on her career, on finding success where she could. It was no wonder she and Estelle weren't close.

And yet, when he'd called, Ally *had* come to her

mother's aid. She'd put her own job, her own life, on hold to deal with her mother's problems. She'd put aside her own old hurts and resentments in order to rescue Estelle.

That was totally different from Claudia. And it was as much as he could have asked for Estelle even before he'd known the whole story. Certainly it was more than he could have asked after learning how rough Ally's childhood had been.

It was no wonder he'd come to admire and respect Ally and all that was beneath the surface.

And it wasn't only the way Ally had stepped up when she'd needed to. There was so much more about her that impressed him. So much more depth than he'd expected to find at the start of this.

The kind of depth that had her looking at things through Estelle's perspective and finding some understanding for her mother's harshness. Feeling compassion for what Estelle had gone through, for what she'd lost, and why she'd responded the way she had.

No, it was no wonder that he'd been disarmed by Ally. No wonder she'd touched on a soft spot in him.

Besides coming through for her mother, she was beautiful, intelligent, quick and clever. She made him laugh. She had insight and wisdom. She was easy to talk to. She was interesting. She was even so down-to-earth that knowing and working with celebrities hadn't seemed to affect her.

And on top of all that, there was something about her

that made him feel as if he was home when he was with her. Something about being with her that had given him the feeling he'd longed for all his life.

That baffled him the most and as he sipped his coffee he turned his back on the window, leaned on the sill and really thought about it.

Home. He'd never really been too sure what that was. It sure as hell hadn't been the foster homes he'd been in—he'd never felt like anything but an interloper in any of those. And the group homes had been worse.

He'd loved being with Nina and Bubby, but again, always with the awareness that he didn't actually belong with them. That he was the outsider they'd let in.

There was just something about being with Ally that made him feel as if he was with the person—the one person—he was supposed to be with.

There was a…a calmness, he guessed, that had come over him. A sense of completion, somehow, when he was with Ally. There was something about being with her that took away his loneliness the way it had never been taken away before.

Damn if he didn't have the feeling that she was what he'd been looking for all his life.

And now that he'd found her, he had to hang on to her.

That realization settled over him like the solution to a puzzle he'd been working on for as long as he could remember. She was his home, his center.

But any minute now she was going to decide what to do about Estelle and—best bet—Ally would go back to

L.A. And there was no way everything he wanted with her, from her, could be had with her there…

"Now you're in dicey territory," he warned himself, pushing off the windowsill and beginning to pace as he felt the need to take action.

Because now not only was there a stake for Estelle in Ally being in Chicago, there was a stake in it for him.

And the stakes were high.

"Nina," he said out loud.

He went to his desk, set his coffee mug down and snatched up the receiver on his phone. Then he dialed his friend's number.

"Nina?" he said when the other end of the line was finally picked up.

"Great minds work alike," Nina said with a laugh, recognizing his voice. "I was just going to call you."

She'd told him on Tuesday that David hadn't been able to talk to Helen before leaving for Japan, but that David would keep trying.

"Were you going to call me with good news, I hope?"

"As a matter of fact," Nina confirmed.

"So they're interested in hiring Ally as designer for the hotels?"

"Hmm… Why do you sound so desperate?"

Jake laughed. "Give me a break" was his only answer.

"What's going on, Jake?"

"More of the same," Jake admitted, knowing Nina well enough to know she'd just get it out of him anyway. "Ally's the one, Nina. She's it for me."

"I knew it! I told Bubby something was different with Ally. I could just feel it."

"So what about the job?" Jake persisted.

"Things are even worse in San Francisco than they thought. The decorator there—Riki—*is* in Thatcher's pocket, plus he's been taking kickbacks and demanding bribes. He's history, but whoever takes over there is not only going to be in a crunch to get the place finished on time, they'll have to deal with some very unhappy suppliers and contractors who have been having the squeeze put on them."

"Not the issue at the moment, Nina," Jake reminded, caring only that what he'd just realized he wanted, needed, be put on track to happen.

"Ooh, you *are* desperate," Nina said with smug satisfaction. "Well, David got hold of Helen late last night and she called me a few minutes ago—that's why I was about to call you. Helen hasn't found a designer she's satisfied with yet, she did some quick investigation into Ally, and is definitely interested in her—although she was surprised that Ally would consider moving here and wants to make sure she knows that that's a must."

It's a must for more than decorating Taka Hotels, Jake thought.

"Did you talk to Ally about this the way I keep telling you to?" Nina asked.

"Not yet," Jake admitted.

"Jake! You should have told her!"

"Isn't it better I break it to her now with good news?"

"Not if she's anything like me." Nina sighed. "Helen wants to meet with Ally as soon as possible."

"Great!"

"It's not a done deal or anything, you know," Nina cautioned.

"Especially since Ally doesn't know I've even put her in the running," Jake muttered. "But it's still a big step in the right direction."

"So when do you think you can get Ally to Helen? Or at least to me so I can get her to Helen?"

Jake checked his appointment book. His afternoon schedule was light. "I think I can clear some space in an hour or so. Any chance maybe Bubby could get Estelle out of the house? Lunch could be on me…"

"Well, if you're paying, I think I might be persuaded to pick up Bubby *and* Estelle, and take them somewhere *really* nice."

Jake laughed again. "Right, stick it to the lovesick jerk."

"Seems only fair," Nina confirmed without conscience.

"Just get Estelle out so I can have Ally to myself to talk her into this."

"Leave it to me," Nina promised like a coconspirator.

"And keep your fingers crossed for me that Ally has rediscovered the appeal of the Windy City."

"I'll keep my fingers crossed that she's discovered the appeal of big, dumb shrinks who are silly for her," Nina teased.

"That, too," Jake confirmed, hanging up and hoping like hell that he really could convince Ally to stay in Chicago.

"You arranged for me to be left out of a fancy lunch with the girls? I hope you have something really good planned to make up for it," Ally said as she and Jake climbed the stairs to her apartment just before one o'clock on Wednesday.

After Tuesday night's lovemaking, Ally had been low energy and full of yawns. Until she'd learned that Jake was having Nina take Estelle and Bubby out to lunch so he could come over, and he and Ally could have some time alone. Then, while Estelle got dressed up, Ally had revamped her own appearance.

She'd taken her hair from its ponytail and brushed it to fall free around her face and shoulders. She'd applied fresh mascara, blush and lip gloss. She'd changed out of the loose-fitting jeans and T-shirt into tighter-fitting versions of both—over much more sexy underwear.

And the yawns she hadn't been able to control all morning? Gone. Knowing Jake was on his way, assuming the fact that he'd made sure they'd have some time to themselves meant more of the many-splendored-lovemaking, had reenergized her completely.

So once they went into her apartment, she closed the door and waited for him to take her into his arms.

Only he didn't.

Instead, he turned to face her and said, "I have some great news. I got you a job offer."

"What are you talking about?" she said in disbelief, stepping close in front of him and placing her hands on that chest that was too magnificent to be hidden behind his shirt and tie.

Jake covered her hands with his, squeezing them, holding them tight. "The Taka hotel chain needs a new designer—and they want you."

It took Ally a moment to take in the information. "The Taka hotel chain?" she repeated.

"There have been complications with their current designer that you can get into with Nina or Helen or—"

"Helen? Who is Helen?"

"Helen Taka-Hanson, David's sister-in-law and one of the heads of the Taka-Hanson hospitality division. Anyway, I suggested you for the job, and there's a very real possibility that they'll hire you. And if they do, you'll be able to move back to Chicago and Estelle won't have to go into assisted living—"

"Wait, *what?*" Ally said to slow him down. "I'll be able to move back to Chicago? I never said—"

"You said you couldn't move back here because relocating would mean reestablishing your business and that would take years. But if you get the Taka job they *want* someone based in Chicago. And not only would you take over the job on their San Francisco hotel and the one that's not quite built yet in Japan, but as I understand it, there are more hotels in the planning, so you'd be instantly established."

"But I didn't say I *wanted* to move back here," she pointed out, stunned by where this was going.

"You said you couldn't do anything else because you didn't have the option of moving back here, that if you did, you'd consider it. But now you *could* have the option, so you *can* consider it, and you *wouldn't* have to move Estelle."

Ally reared back slightly. "So not only have you gotten me a job that relocates me, you also think I should live with my mother?"

He smiled a crooked smile and Ally tried not to be influenced by how incredibly handsome he was.

"Actually, that gets into part two," he said.

"Part two," she echoed him again.

"Part two is you and me."

She liked the sound of that better, but she was still wary. "Okay… What about you and me?" she asked.

His smile turned soft and warm as he told her how his opinion of her had changed since they'd met, that he admired everything she'd done with her mother.

How important she'd become to him. That she'd filled the gap that had been in his life. That she was actually who he'd been looking for all along.

"This morning," he concluded, "it hit me. The way I feel about you… I've never felt this way about anyone else. I've never felt this way about *being* with anyone else. I just knew in my gut that you and I have been following our own separate paths just so we could be led to each other now. Everything you said about your mother and father and what they meant to each other? How important they were to each other? That's how I feel about you, Ally. No, I don't want our kids to be left out in the cold by it—I want them embraced by it and included in it—but beyond that, what your parents had together is how I want it to be with you and me."

Ally just stared up at him, more stunned than she had been a moment earlier over the job issue. Stunned and confused by conflicting feelings of her own—half of them fed by words that were wonderful to hear, the other half outraged by the liberties he was taking. The liberties he'd *already* taken.

But he just went on taking them. "I know this is whirlwind," he said. "And I know you have work commitments you'd still have to finish up in L.A., not to mention that there would be travel involved in decorating the hotels. But the thing is, if we're together, we could build a place of our own right here. One or both of us would be near enough to take care of Estelle so she wouldn't have to move. Plus, I could help you work through all that old baggage with your mother and mend the tear in your relationship so we could all share Estelle's last years as a family—"

"*Whoa!* Wait! Wow!"

That had come from the outraged half but she hadn't been able to stop it. She'd just needed to stop him.

She pulled her hands out from under his and stepped

away from him. "It's barely been half a day since I saw you last and you've closed down my business in L.A., opened one in Chicago with a major new client that needs entire *hotels* decorated, built a house that has me basically living with my mother, moved yourself into it, *and* you think you can make Estelle and me best friends?"

He grinned. "Too much all at once?"

He was joking, but Ally saw no humor in the situation. He had so thoroughly mapped out her entire future without even consulting her.

"To start with, I can't believe you put me up for a job—a *huge,* career-altering, change-my-whole-life job—without even *mentioning* it to me."

"I wanted to find out if it was a possibility before I got your hopes up."

"You didn't even know that it *would* get my hopes up, that I'd even *want* to do something like design for a hotel chain!"

His grin faded and his eyebrows rose in surprise. "This is a good thing. I've solved all your problems."

"I can solve my own problems! For instance, today it occurred to me that I could do some remodeling on this apartment and get someone to come in and look after Mother in exchange for a free place to live—*that* is a solution to a problem. What you're doing is the same thing you did on the phone when you first called me and again when I got here—you're giving me orders, making demands, telling me what I have to do!"

He frowned. "That's *not* what I'm doing."

"Yes, you are, Jake! You've decided *what* should happen, *how* it should happen and you've gone behind my back to *make* it happen."

"I just listened to what you said and acted accordingly," he said defensively. "I thought I was helping. I thought you'd already started to see Estelle in a new light, to have some sympathy for her. I thought you were serious about disrupting her life now because you couldn't be here to take care of her." He ran a hand through his hair. "I thought if you had the chance, you could come back here and take it the rest of the way, that you could get to know each other as adults, repair the relationship—"

"You just can't resist pushing the family thing, can you?" Ally shot at him. Everything he was saying *was* true, but it still felt as if he was putting unreasonable expectations on her.

He didn't answer that. "I also thought that we really had connected. Fast, yes, but I thought we'd made the kind of connection that happens fast because it's right, because it's meant to be, because it's destined…"

That sounded good, too. But still, she couldn't just let Jake completely and totally change her life without having so much as offered her a choice in the matter.

And what kind of a life would it be, anyway, with someone who was always so convinced that he had all the answers? That his way was the only way? Especially when she was feeling at that moment the way he'd made her feel at the start of this—backed into a corner, bossed around, overwhelmed, not sure exactly what was going on or if she could deal with it or...

"No!" she heard herself shout, then collected herself. "It isn't meant to be that I take orders about the direction my life should go in."

"In the first place," he said with deadly calm, obviously having become as angry as she was. "I'm not *telling* you what job to take or where to live or how to live there or what should happen between you and Estelle. I'm telling you what I've done to facilitate what I thought you were leaning towards. I'm offering to try to help ease the two of you into a better relationship with each other."

He shook his head fatalistically and his voice got lower. "And in the second place," he added, "I'm telling you what I want. Which—by the way—I said last night, if you'll recall, when I said I wanted more than a fling with you."

"What you *didn't* say was that you wanted to control me and that you'd already taken steps to accomplish it."

That one made him madder. She saw it in the broad shoulders that squared themselves, in the darkening of his charcoal-colored eyes. Then she heard it in the tightness of his voice.

"I'm not trying to control you. Like I said, I thought I was helping you. I also thought I wasn't the only one to see a future for us. But apparently I was wrong."

He stepped around her, returned to the apartment door and opened it.

But before he left he turned back. "Just in case you're

interested in the business opportunity—Helen Taka-Hanson wants to talk to you as soon as possible. Nina can put you in touch with her. Otherwise, you can tell Nina to let Helen know you aren't interested."

Then, before Ally had even turned around, he was gone.

And Ally was too angry to care.

Or at least that was what she told herself.

Chapter Fourteen

Ally was in a daze. Her stomach was one big knot. She'd been on the verge of tears since five minutes after Jake had walked out of the apartment and was worried that, at any moment, she could spontaneously burst out crying without provocation. She was miserable and confused and furious and nauseous and in more emotional pain than she'd been in since her father had been killed.

So, she asked herself, what was she doing late Wednesday afternoon, sitting in Nina's living room across from Helen Taka-Hanson?

I must have lost my mind...

It was Nina who had persuaded her. Ally had been waiting when Nina brought Estelle and Bubby back from lunch. Ally had told Jake's friend that she wasn't interested in the job with Taka Hotels.

Nina hadn't pushed. But she *had* pointed out that the job was a big opportunity and asked if Ally was sure she didn't want to at least talk it over with Helen.

Ally's business acumen had kicked in. Regardless of how this had come about, she hadn't been able to deny that it was a great opportunity. The kind that any designer would jump at.

So she'd agreed to meet Helen Taka-Hanson. And Nina had arranged for that meeting right then, before Ally could change her mind.

But even trying to force herself into business mode didn't take away the awful feelings Jake had roused in her and then left her to.

"I did some research on you," Helen began.

When Nina had taken Estelle and Bubby into the kitchen to leave Ally and Helen alone, Helen had insisted that Ally call her by her first name, and had surprised Ally with how down-to-earth, warm, open and friendly she was. Sitting in Nina's living room, Helen was dressed in a flowered sundress and sandals. Ally would never have pegged her for one of the heads of an international company.

"I liked what I saw and heard about you," Helen continued. "Maggie McShane, in particular, gave you an outstanding recommendation."

Ally nodded. "I did her Malibu house last year," she confirmed.

"I don't know if you've heard, but Maggie has agreed to have her wedding at the Taka San Francisco as a soft-opening fete."

"I read about that in the newspaper," Ally said.

"It will be a media event and of course we would want the designer to help with it from an aesthetic standpoint, in addition to designing the interiors."

"That makes sense," Ally agreed.

"Let me tell you a little about the position we're in," Helen said then. "Riki—do you know him?"

"I've heard of him, of course, but we've never met. I've admired his designs, though."

"I'm glad to hear that! Because the San Francisco site is so near to opening, we'll need whoever takes over to pick up where Riki left off and make as few changes as possible. Riki has already caused horrible cost overruns and purposely put us so far behind schedule that in order to make the opening there will have to be a lot of overtime paid out, so sticking to his plans is a must. But after that—beginning with the Kyoto site—you would be able to start from scratch with your own design concepts. I know working with another designer's vision is asking a lot, and I apologize for it, but we're in a bind and of course wherever your own tastes can be implemented without increasing costs would be fine."

Ally nodded her understanding.

"My other sticking point is that I need someone based in Chicago. My husband, Mori, and I divide our time between here and Japan where his family home is, and it just gets too complicated for me to be working from more than two places."

"I can see how it would."

"I know you're based in L.A., but David said there was reason to believe that you might be moving here?"

It was still staggering to hear how far-reaching Jake's machinations had gone behind her back—Nina, David Hanson, Helen Taka-Hanson—all before Ally herself had had any clue that anything was going on or what he had up his sleeve.

But she couldn't dwell on that in the middle of a business meeting, so she forced herself to concentrate.

"My mother is aging and seems to need more help from me than she used to," Ally said ambiguously.

"So you *would* consider relocating your business?"

"This offer would certainly be an incentive," Ally answered.

She knew she wasn't being very convincing, or doing anything to sell herself or her services, that this was about the worst presentation she'd ever made at an interview, but at that point, feeling the way she did, she was doing the best she could. Besides, she *wasn't* sure she was willing to move back to Chicago. Especially when it meant that she would have been so successfully manipulated.

Helen went on to talk about how much travel would be involved in being the exclusive designer for the Taka hotel chain, and Ally assured her that traveling to her clients' locations was something she was accustomed to.

They discussed the kind of overall styles and themes

that might come up for future projects, but Helen seemed to have no doubt that Ally's abilities were versatile enough to vary from eclectic to traditional to whatever else might be asked of her down the line.

Helen had already done enough investigation into her to know that not only were her artistic talents well respected and admired, but that she was considered reliable, responsible, that she brought things in on time, often under budget, and always with professionalism.

"All in all," Helen concluded, "I didn't hear a single negative thing about you, I'm impressed with what I've seen of your work, and if you're willing to change your home base, I think we could do business."

In a day full of unexpectedness, this was just one more. Ally hadn't thought she would be offered the position on the spot.

And she was hardly at her sharpest, so she knew it was clear that she was taken aback by that.

But Helen merely smiled serenely and said, "I know you'll need to think it over. I'd only ask that you not take too much time."

"No," Ally said, hating how dim-witted she sounded. "I won't. I know you need someone right away."

"We really do. Which was why I was so thrilled to learn that I might actually have the chance to get someone of your caliber, with your credentials and uncommon talent at such short notice. I'm just hoping it's fate that's made you even consider coming back to Chicago right now, when we so desperately need you."

Fate, destiny—it was a day full of that, too, wasn't it?

But once more Ally focused on matters at hand.

"I appreciate the offer…" she said, giving herself the option of saying no right there and then. Of thwarting Jake's grand scheme and showing him that she was not some kind of puppet with strings that he could just pull to suit himself.

But something kept her from doing that.

Probably her business sense again, she told herself. Probably nothing at all that had to do with Jake Fox.

"I promise I'll think seriously—and quickly—about your offer," she added.

"Good," Helen countered, standing then to signal that the interview—however casual—had come to an end. "I'm going to have to get going, I'm due for a conference call in half an hour."

She raised her voice enough to be heard in the kitchen, and Nina, Bubby and Estelle rejoined them to say goodbye.

Ally stayed in the background for most of that.

Because while she had just received a flattering review and the best job offer of her career, for no reason she could put a finger on, she was wrestling with those tears all over again.

"What's wrong?"

Estelle had barely waited until Ally was behind the steering wheel to ask.

They were just leaving Nina's place and Ally thought

that keeping herself from crying had hidden the fact that she was upset. Apparently it hadn't.

Still, she said, "Nothing's wrong. I just have a lot to think about."

"Something happened while I was at lunch. Something with Jake," Estelle persisted. "You were all smiles over him coming to the house, but since I got back you've had the mopes. Did you fight with him?"

"Yes," Ally said. Denying it seemed useless.

"Nina said it was Jake who got you that interview with that hotel bigwig this afternoon," Estelle informed her.

Ally sighed. "It was his idea, yes."

"You didn't want it?"

"It wasn't my idea."

"Does everything have to be your idea?"

Ally tried to maintain her calm in response to her mother's familiar critical, challenging tone. "No, everything doesn't have to be my idea. But when it comes to my job, my career, my future, my family and where I end up living, I think I should be considered and asked how I feel about things before anything gets started."

"Your family," Estelle said, picking out that single item on Ally's list. "Does Jake have ideas for me?"

"As a matter of fact he does," Ally confirmed. Then, under her breath, she added, "He has ideas for all of us."

Estelle ignored that. Instead, she said, "Nina hinted around that there's things going on with you and Jake. I know what I've seen—I'd say there is, too."

"Not anymore," Ally said decisively.

She didn't *feel* as decisive as she made it sound, though.

"Nina said that for you to take that hotel job you'd have to live here," Estelle continued. "Do you want to live here again?"

"That's one of the things I'm thinking about."

"Because you don't really want to live too close to me. I understand that. But I wouldn't bother you—if that's what you're worried about."

Ally took her eyes off the road to glance at her mother, feeling guilty for ever giving Estelle the impression that she didn't want to be bothered with her. "I'm not worried about that. Living closer to you would actually work out better for both you and me."

Estelle seemed surprised by that answer. "I know I'd like it better," she admitted as if it was difficult for her to say it.

That was a surprise. "You would?"

"I see the way Bubby and Nina are together. It's nice. I wonder if we could have that, too. If I could make up for things I said and did that I shouldn't have."

"That would be nice," Ally said quietly.

"So what's complicating things, if it isn't that you don't want to move back here?" the older woman asked.

"It's just...complicated, that's all."

"You wouldn't jump at the opportunity to be with Jake?"

It really *must* have been obvious that something was going on between them.

"Jake can be pushy. And manipulative," Ally said, her own frustration with him bubbling to the surface. "He makes up his mind, he decides the way something should be done, and that's it! He barrels in and tries to force it to be done that way."

"He can be strong willed," Estelle agreed. "I know he was driving me crazy about all that medical business before you came. I guess he was right, but still—"

"His way isn't always the *only* right way. And he butts in to things he doesn't have any business butting in to."

"Like your work," Estelle said.

"Yes, like my work."

"So you wish he wouldn't have gotten you that interview today."

"Not without talking to me about it first."

"If you don't want the job, then why did you even go talk to that woman?"

"I didn't say I don't want the job. Jake just had no business doing what he did and making such grand assumptions."

"And that's what made you mad at him?"

"Yes."

But it felt so much bigger than what her mother was reducing it to. Especially when she wasn't merely mad at him, when she'd turned down his plans for a future for them together, when she'd ended things with him...

"So get over it and make up with him and stop moping," Estelle decreed.

That sounded like the old Estelle, and Ally responded in kind. "Can you just this once be on my side?" she shouted.

She felt rather than saw her mother slowly pivot her head in her direction. She knew the glare she would face if she looked at Estelle, so she kept her eyes on the road and merely did what she knew would be required.

"I'm sorry. I just don't want to talk about this."

But of course that wasn't enough to keep her mother from pursuing it. Although when she did she again shocked Ally with a kind, patient, motherly tone of voice.

"I'm always on your side, Alice."

Ally did glance at her mother now because she couldn't believe the lack of anger. Of recrimination. And her mother's expression matched the tone—she honestly wasn't outraged by Ally losing her temper.

"This is just complicated," Ally repeated. "It's probably better not to talk about it."

Estelle respected that and returned to looking out the windshield.

Neither of them spoke for about half a mile.

Then her mother said, "You and Jake. I thought you were like Mitchie and me. I thought it was nice that you found each other."

Once more, surprise caused Ally to look at her mother. "What made you think that?"

Estelle shrugged. "That's just what it seemed like.

First the fighting and you didn't like him—like Mitchie and me. Then a little at a time you started to like him, he started to like you. Then there was him spending last night—don't think I didn't know about that."

Ally flinched. "How?"

"I got up at five-thirty this morning to go to the bathroom and I looked out front and his car was still there. Then lo and behold, it was gone an hour later when I got up for the day. I wasn't born yesterday. And you better not be doing that with just anybody. You better have strong feelings for him and an eye to a future."

Ally decided against making a comment.

"I want you to be happy, Alice," Estelle said, in a gentle tone Ally had never heard. "I like Jake and he deserves to be happy, too. You could be good for each other."

Not given the way she was feeling at that moment...

"So what if he was bossy?" Estelle reasoned. "You must've stood up to him and set him straight. You want somebody who can think for himself, don't you? Sean had to have his family around to make a committee decision out of everything. You wouldn't have that problem with Jake."

"Even without one, Jake is still all about family," Ally muttered.

Her mother heard it anyway. "Only, *you'd* be Jake's family, so *you'd* come first. Not like with Sean."

They'd reached home and Ally pulled into the driveway and turned off the engine.

But Estelle was obviously not finished saying what

she had to say because as they walked to the house, she picked up where she'd left off.

"And I'll tell you another thing—if you think you aren't going to have to fight some fights with any man, you have another thought coming. That's what men do. They come in and think they have to rule the roost and solve all the problems. Sometimes it's good, sometimes it's a pain in the neck. But just because the idea was his instead of yours, don't cut off your nose to spite your face. You like that man or you wouldn't be moping, so no matter what he did, fight for whatever you need to fight for and get over it."

"It isn't that easy," Ally said.

"It isn't if you're making it harder. But here's what I think—for me, being happy was being with Mitchie. And unless I'm seeing things, I think for you, being happy is being with Jake. The rest you can work out if you just aren't stubborn." Estelle clasped Ally's arm in a warm, comforting squeeze and smiled sympathetically. "Now go to your room and think about it."

Her mother's touch brought tears to Ally's eyes, but Estelle's words made her laugh. Her mother was sending her to her room as if she were a child who merely needed a time-out to think about what she'd done wrong.

But she did need a time-out, so once she had her mother inside, Ally went out the back door and climbed the steps to her apartment, where memories of Jake waited.

Wonderful memories of him the night before. Not so wonderful memories of him from this afternoon.

All of them hard to bear now.

Unless maybe—difficult as it was for her to believe or admit—her mother was right.

Chapter Fifteen

After leaving her mother in the house late Wednesday afternoon, Ally opened her windows, turned on her fans, kicked off her shoes and flopped down on her neatly made bed.

Then she thought again about Jake and how they'd spent the night in that bed and she bounced back up as if it were made of thorns.

Instead, she went to the sofa.

Sitting sideways—feet up—gave her a view of the bed and that wasn't much better. But she didn't have the energy to move again, so she stayed where she was. And moped.

Yes, her mother was right about the moping. But was she also right about everything else? Ally asked herself.

Historically, her mother had never considered Ally's problems to be as serious as Ally had considered them. So Ally was accustomed to her mother reducing and diminishing what was important to her and didn't generally take Estelle's views to heart.

But this time?

This time, if her mother was right...

Only, she *wasn't* right about it all, Ally thought defensively. Everything did *not* have to be her own idea. She'd used suggestions from the decorators who worked with her, she'd used ideas from her clients. She wasn't upset and angry with Jake merely because the job with Taka Hotels had been his idea rather than hers.

It was the going-behind-her-back, the arranging and planning for her entire future without even asking her opinion.

A future that—ironically—she might end up with anyway if she took the job with Taka Hotels and moved back to Chicago.

Great, now she was going back and forth in her own head as if she were arguing with her mother.

But it was true—she *had* gone to the interview. She *had* been offered the job. And it *was* a great opportunity that could put her back here where she could avoid sending her mother to assisted living—all the things Jake had outlined.

Without the parts that had included him...

Unless she did as her mother had encouraged her to do.

Again with the back-and-forth.

But her mother's words echoed in her mind just the same. *Get over it*—that had been Estelle's edict. Get over being mad at Jake, get over what he'd done without even consulting her, get over it.

And if she did, maybe she could have those other parts of the future that included him…

"And then what?" she challenged herself out loud. "A whole life of him telling me what to do, when to do it and how to do it the way he has been since day one?"

Because he *had* even given her orders the very first time she'd spoken to him, before they'd so much as set eyes on each other.

Although between the call that had initially brought her home and getting her that interview with Helen Taka-Hanson today, she had to concede that he hadn't shown any signs of being bossy or manipulative. In fact, he'd left everything she'd done and considered doing with her mother up to her, even when she knew he couldn't have been thrilled her options.

So maybe the bossy, manipulative things weren't so much major flaws as they were something else?

Was it possible that her mother was right and it was just that male thing? That Jake had only been playing Mr. Fix-It whether she needed things fixed or not?

To be fair, she guessed she *had* needed him to be forceful to get her out here in the first place. She hadn't known anything was going on with her mother's health, and Estelle would certainly never have told her. Had Jake not called and insisted that she come to Chicago, it probably would have taken a call from police or a hospital to convince her that she had to drop what she was doing and come home.

So he'd seen the need and used what force he'd had to solve the problem.

She supposed she couldn't fault him for that. And as for manipulative, he hadn't manipulated anything on that count—he'd been straightforward about what actions she had to take, albeit loudly.

But this today with Taka Hotels? That hadn't been so straightforward.

Of course, all he'd done was get her the interview. He hadn't accepted the job or put her in a position where damage could be done if she didn't take it. And she could have refused to talk to Helen Taka-Hanson. She could have nixed the whole plan before it was ever set into motion. So maybe that wasn't quite as manipulative as it had seemed before.

And the rest of what he'd presented to her at lunchtime? Okay, she had to admit that the rest had only been suggestions about what could happen if she did take the job and move back here. And what he'd dumped on her today hadn't only been setting up appointments for her mother's medical tests, or visiting assisted-living facilities with her. What he'd dumped on her today had been stepping over the line.

Oh, she knew what her mother would say to that! Estelle would say that it was all right when he played Mr. Fix-It with things she *wanted* his help on, but she'd condemned him when he did the same for other, more personal things, so how was he supposed to know when it was all right and when it wasn't?

Maybe *that* was when that fight-the-fights thing Estelle had suggested kicked in. Assuming, of course, that anything would ever kick in again between the two of them.

But actually, she *had* fought some of that fight today, Ally reasoned. Because certainly Jake had left knowing that she felt he'd gone too far.

But would he go that far again if he had the chance? she wondered. Because with Sean, she'd fought the fights but it hadn't mattered—nothing would ever have changed.

So, what if fighting the fights with Jake didn't make any difference either?

But somehow, now that she'd stopped thinking about Jake as bossy and manipulative, and recognized that what he'd been doing all along was trying to help and problem solve the way he'd claimed today, it didn't seem like something that would be ever present, the way the family issue with Sean had been. And if she *was* involved with Jake, when problems arose, she would be fair warned that it was his nature to rush in and find a solution, so if she made sure to encourage him to talk over with her whatever he was thinking about, wouldn't that help? Wouldn't even Mr. Fix-It be inclined to want to do whatever it took to solve the problem of jumping in too quickly and too forcefully to solve problems?

It seemed likely.

Actually, it seemed as if she could use his Mr. Fix-It tendencies to advantage in this.

"Hmm..." she said, feeling suddenly relieved that she might have just found a way to use what she'd thought was an obstacle—much like finding a way to use a built-in eyesore in a room she was designing.

But did this mean that she really was considering what Jake had laid out to her today?

Closing her business in L.A.

Moving back to Chicago.

Living within shouting distance of her mother.

Dealing daily with Estelle, with Estelle's aging, with Estelle's health...

Ally wilted beneath the weight of merely thinking about what all of that would entail.

And Jake was *volunteering* to get in on it?

Maybe he was out of his mind.

But as overwhelming as it all was to her, considering the situation with Jake in the picture cast an entirely different light on it.

If closing her business in L.A. and moving back to Chicago meant being with him, it had its own special appeal.

If living here meant being in a place where she and Jake could spend every night the way they had last night? That possibility gave her a rush that raised goose bumps on her arms.

And if she wanted to keep her mother out of assisted living, that was aided tremendously by having a second person to help carry the load, to be here when she couldn't be. And she'd already experienced how—with Jake's help, support and tempering influence—she could deal with Estelle and make their relationship better. And more than that, even enjoy Estelle the way she had when the three of them had been together for the backyard barbecue, for Nina's dinner party, for the evening of the Follies at the senior center. Because with Jake around, she actually saw a new side of her mother, a fun side that she liked. So in essence, he'd already begun to help their relationship improve.

And there was something else that Ally had to admit that her mother had been right about.

The most important thing Estelle had said.

Something that, now that Ally's anger was disappearing, she was coming to realize herself.

For her, being happy *did* mean being with Jake.

She'd already recognized that being with him had had the power to lighten her mood, to make her feel good, to make her laugh even at the worst of times. And now she knew that the reason for that was that he *was* for her what her father had been for her mother—just the way he'd said earlier. That they *could* have what her parents had had together.

And that was worth everything. Worth every change she would have to make, every adjustment, every alteration.

It was even worth every fight she might have to fight.

Her mother was right about one other thing, she thought then.

That she and Jake could be a family. The family Jake had never had, the family he'd always wanted but held out for. The one that she'd wanted, too.

At least she thought that was what he'd been talking about. She hadn't let him get far enough to be sure...

"I made a mess of this," she groaned, dropping her head to the back of the sofa and closing her eyes.

Just then there was a knock on her door.

Startled, her eyes shot open again, and she yanked her head off the cushion.

She thought it must be her mother, but since she'd installed the intercom, if Estelle wanted or needed her, she'd merely shout into it. Why would she have come all the way outside and up the stairs now?

Ally got off the couch and went to the door. But when she opened it and saw Jake on the landing, she wasn't sure how to react.

"What are you doing here?"

"Your mother called me a few minutes ago and said there was an emergency. But when I got here there was a note on the front door telling me to come to your place..."

"No wonder the two of you like each other—you both decide what I should do and then go ahead and do it yourselves," Ally muttered, not appreciating that she was facing him before she'd figured out how to do it with aplomb.

"There's no emergency?" Jake demanded, his heartbreakingly handsome features pulled into a worried frown.

"No, there's no emergency." Ally hesitated, mentally stumbling over what to say. "But…I'm glad you're here."

He didn't respond to that except to raise a questioning eyebrow at her.

"Will you come in?" she asked.

He shrugged as if it didn't matter to him one way or another. But as he stepped inside, it struck Ally that he was someone who had gone through his whole life being abandoned and disappointed by people. He'd clearly learned to be self-protective, and she thought that was what he was doing now—cloaking himself in that I-don't-give-a-damn attitude.

But he *had* rushed over here the minute her mother called him, Ally reminded herself. So he must give a damn…

She spotted her mother spying out the kitchen window just before she closed the door behind them.

When she turned around she found that Jake had put some distance between them—he'd moved to the center of her small apartment.

He was standing with his hands on his hips, his weight on one leg more than the other, looking like the stern, serious Jake he'd been when they'd first met. He still didn't say anything, though, obviously unwilling to give an inch.

But it was her mother who had made the bogus emergency call to get him there, so it seemed only right that she be the one to break the ice.

"I'm sorry, I didn't know Mother had called you," she began. "I told her what happened with us earlier and she thought I should just get over it and patch things up with you—"

"So she got me over here under false pretenses?"

"I guess so. I didn't know she was doing anything—I left her in the house... I needed some time alone to think," she added haltingly. "I didn't even hear her over the intercom. Although I don't know how she made a phone call without my hearing it, I've heard every other one she's made..."

"Apparently she's well enough now to be wily," he said, but with a hint of sarcasm that let Ally know he didn't entirely believe that.

What did he think, that she'd been in on some plot with her mother to get him here?

But at that moment that was probably the lesser issue, she told herself, letting go of it to get to what was more important.

"It's good that you came, though," she reiterated. "It saved me having to go out and find you."

Jake waited, encouraging nothing.

"I'm not saying that I appreciate what you did with the whole Taka Hotels thing or that I'm okay—or would or will ever be okay—with you making decisions that include me without talking to me about them first," she said. "But I might have reacted differently if you had handled it differently."

She wasn't going to concede more than that because

she didn't want to send the message that he could ever do that again.

"Anyway, it's Mother's opinion," she concluded, "that you really were only trying to be helpful and after thinking about it, I decided that might be true."

"Which is what I told you myself," he pointed out. But his tone wasn't quite as stilted or angry.

"Jake, regardless of what your intentions were, your method was what caused the problem," she said. "And I don't want to be told how everything is going to be without having any say in it."

"You're right," he said, surprising her when she'd expected him to yell back at her. "I just got so caught up in what I wanted and how I thought I could make it work, that I didn't stop to think about anything but presenting you with a flawless plan you couldn't refuse."

"So it wasn't *only* that you were trying to help and solve my problems."

"There was that, too. For your sake and for Estelle's. But I'm only human, Ally. I saw what I wanted—you— and I did what I thought would get it for me. If I was too gung ho it was because I didn't want there to be any holes you could slip through. I guess all I succeeded at was making you feel trapped."

"Maybe a little," she agreed. "But you succeeded at more than that." She went on to tell him about her meeting with Helen Taka-Hanson and the job offer. And the fact that she thought she was going to accept it.

"It really is a solution," she admitted. "And I have to say it's an incredible opportunity. But only one of them."

"Okay," he said, sounding confused.

"The rest of them are up to you."

"Okay," he repeated.

"The biggest one is that you have to promise me that you won't ever leave me out of the decision-making process again. That I have a say in *how* the problems are solved."

"Done."

Said like a true problem solver.

Ally had to fight a smile.

"The rest involves the things you suggested earlier—building a place of our own here, lending a hand with Mother so I can do the traveling I'll need to…that stuff."

Jake took two steps forward, putting him nearer to her. "The stuff like marrying me?"

"I never heard that particular solution," she pointed out, a thrill slowly spreading through her.

"Maybe because I was planning to ask you that after I'd shown you how it could work out. But you didn't give me the chance."

"I'm giving it to you now," she said.

"Gee, thanks," he answered, smiling.

But he took another step, coming close enough to wrap his arms around her waist and pull her to him.

"Ally Rogers," he said solemnly then. "Will you marry me?"

"Let me get this straight," she said instead of giving him a simple yes. "You're not only willing to marry me, but you're also okay with living in a house hooked onto my mother's, and living with your mother-in-law, who would happen to be the cantankerous and difficult Estelle Rogers?"

"Sounds like heaven to me," he said with a half grin.

"Having this family might change your mind about how great it is to be a part of one," she warned.

"I still want it. For better or worse. I want *you.* I want kids with you. I want to spend the rest of my life with you."

"Then yes—even though I have reason to doubt your sanity—I will marry you."

Jake's half grin broadened into a full one that reminded Ally of a kid on Christmas morning. Then he kissed her. A deep, deep kiss that melted her insides.

Her arms went around him as his lips parted over hers, as hers parted in answer and welcomed his tongue with glee.

Oh, how she loved this man!

Only in that moment did she fully accept just how much and know that no matter what, she would have had to knock down whatever obstacles had separated them because she loved him too much to lose him.

As if he knew what was going through her mind, he ended that kiss and said, "I love you, Ally. More than I thought it was possible to love anyone."

"I love you, too—that's what I was just thinking."

"I'll tell you what else I was thinking," he added

then, his dark coal-colored eyes casting a glance in the direction of her bed.

Ally groaned. "As much as I would like that…I just saw Mother peeking out the kitchen window when I let you in. She could come up here any minute to make sure I'm doing what she wants. And I don't think *that*—" she nodded toward the bed "—is what she wants. She already knows you spent last night and it didn't get her stamp of approval."

"How does she know I spent last night?"

"I guess she got up to get a drink and we both slept through it. She saw your car."

"We're going to have to check those intercoms."

"But for now…"

Jake smiled slyly. "You don't want her seeing more than my car."

"Do you?"

He laughed. "Not particularly. So here's what we'll do—we'll go down—"

"You're *telling* me?"

"Sorry." He rephrased. "*How about* if we go down, tell her the good news, take her out to a celebratory dinner—"

"Asking is so much better than telling," Ally commended him. "But what if Mother has another coupon? Remember the last dinner to celebrate that she wasn't seriously ill…"

Jake laughed. "I'll put my foot down—no coupons or buffets no matter how much free coffee she gets. This will be our *engagement* dinner. And if it's an *engagement* dinner that gives us the excuse to ply her with a lot of champagne so she comes home and sleeps like a baby."

"You really do have some good ideas," Ally said, grinning herself now.

"Here's another one—maybe after we've softened Estelle up with a little liquor we'll let her know that even before we can actually tie the knot, I'm going to be living here with you…"

"I'll let you go ahead and tell her *that,*" Ally said with a laugh, just imagining her mother's reaction.

Jake kissed her again—another, even better kiss that very nearly put Ally far enough over the edge of wanting him to be willing to run the risk of her mother walking in on them making love.

Until, just in the nick of time, Jake ended that kiss, too.

"Later," he said in a passion-raspy voice that let her know he was teetering on the edge himself.

But instead of letting go of her so they could leave the apartment—and temptation—behind, Jake pulled her tight against him, holding her head to his chest with one big hand cupped to the back of it.

"I do love you, Ally," he said again.

"I love you, Jake," she said.

"It's you and me forever, you know?" he whispered into her hair.

"I wouldn't have it any other way," she said quietly. And she meant it.

Because with Jake by her side, she felt as if she could handle anything.

And if ever something came up that she couldn't handle?

She knew he would be right there to help her. Or support her. Or comfort her. Or distract her.

For better or worse.

But as she stood there drinking in the feel of those powerful arms around her, she somehow just knew that it would always be for better.

* * * * *

*Look for the next installment in the
new Special Edition continuity*
BACK IN BUSINESS
*Movie star Maggie McShane always wanted
her own happily-ever-after.
But a sudden breakup leaves her with a
broken heart—until a sexy rancher offers to
help her pick up the pieces.
Has the big-screen Cinderella finally met
her Prince Charming in cowboy boots?
Don't miss*
THE RANCHER'S SURPRISE MARRIAGE
By
*Susan Crosby
On sale September 2008,
wherever Silhouette Books are sold.*

The Colton family is back!
Enjoy a sneak preview of
COLTON'S SECRET SERVICE
by Marie Ferrarella, part of
THE COLTONS: FAMILY FIRST *miniseries.*
Available from Silhouette Romantic Suspense
in September 2008.

He cautioned himself to be leery. He was human and he'd been conned before. But never by anyone nearly so attractive. Never by anyone he'd felt so attracted to.

In her defense, Nick supposed that Georgie could actually be telling him the truth. That she was a victim in all this. He had his people back in California checking her out, to make sure she was who she said she was and had, as she claimed, not even been near a computer but on the road these last few months that the threats had been made.

In the meantime, he was doing his own checking out. Up close and exceedingly personal. So personal he could feel his blood stirring.

It had been a long time since he'd thought of himself

as anything other than a law enforcement agent of one type or other. But Georgeann Grady made him remember that beneath the oaths he had taken and his devotion to duty, there beat the heart of a man.

A man who'd been far too long without the touch of a woman.

He watched as the light from the fireplace caressed the outline of Georgie's small, trim, jean-clad body as she moved about the rustic living room that could have easily come off the set of a Hollywood Western. Except that it was genuine.

As genuine as she claimed to be?

Something inside of him hoped so.

He wasn't supposed to be taking sides. His only interest in being here was to guarantee Senator Joe Colton's safety as the latter continued to make his bid for the presidency. Everything else was supposed to be secondary, but, Nick had to silently admit, that was just a wee bit hard to remember right now.

Earlier, before she'd put her precocious handful of a daughter to bed, Georgie had fed his appetite by whipping up some kind of a delicious concoction out of the vegetables she'd pulled from her garden. Vegetables that, by all rights, should have been withered and dried. She'd mentioned that a friend came by on occasion to weed and tend it. Still, it surprised him that somehow she'd managed to make something mouthwatering out of it.

Almost as mouthwatering as she looked to him right at this moment.

Again, he was reminded of the appetite that hadn't been fed, hadn't been satisfied.

And wasn't going to be, Nick sternly told himself. At least not now. Maybe later, when things took on a more definite shape and all the questions in his head were answered to his satisfaction, there would be time to explore this feeling. This woman. But not now.

Damn it.

"Sorry about the lack of light," Georgie said, breaking into his train of thought as she turned around to face him. If she noticed the way he was looking at her, she gave no indication. "But I don't see a point in paying for electricity if I'm not going to be here. Besides, Emmie really enjoys camping out. She likes roughing it."

"And you?" Nick asked, moving closer to her, so close that a whisper would have trouble fitting in. "What do you like?"

The very breath stopped in Georgie's throat as she looked up at him.

"I think you've got a fair shot of guessing that one," she told him softly.

* * * * *

Romantic
SUSPENSE

Sparked by Danger,
Fueled by Passion.

The Coltons Are Back!

Marie Ferrarella
Colton's Secret Service

The Coltons: Family First

On a mission to protect a senator, Secret Service agent
Nick Sheffield tracks down a threatening message only
to discover Georgie Gradie Colton, a rodeo-riding single
mom, who insists on her innocence. Nick is instantly
taken with the feisty redhead, but vows not to let his
feelings interfere with his mission. Now he must figure
out if this woman is conning him or if he can trust her
and the passion they share....

Available September wherever books are sold.

Look for upcoming Colton titles
from Silhouette Romantic Suspense:

RANCHER'S REDEMPTION by Beth Cornelison, Available October
THE SHERIFF'S AMNESIAC BRIDE by Linda Conrad, Available November
SOLDIER'S SECRET CHILD by Caridad Piñeiro, Available December
BABY'S WATCH by Justine Davis, Available January 2009
A HERO OF HER OWN by Carla Cassidy, Available February 2009

Visit Silhouette Books at www.eHarlequin.com   SRS27598

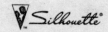

SPECIAL EDITION

HEART OF STONE
by
DIANA PALMER

On sale September.

SAVE $1.⁰⁰ OFF

**the Silhouette Special Edition® novel
HEART OF STONE on sale
September 2008, when you purchase
2 Silhouette Special Edition® books.**

*Available wherever books are sold, including most
bookstores, supermarkets, drugstores and discount stores.*

Coupon expires December 31, 2008. Redeemable at participating
retail outlets in the U.S. only. Limit one coupon per customer.

U.S. RETAILERS: Harlequin Enterprises Limited will pay the face value of this coupon plus
8¢ if submitted by customer for this specified product only. Any other use constitutes fraud.
Coupon is nonassignable. Void if taxed, prohibited or restricted by law. Consumer must pay
any government taxes. Void if copied. For reimbursement submit coupons and proof of sales
directly to Harlequin Enterprises Limited, P.O. Box 880478, El Paso, TX 88588-0478, U.S.A.
Cash value 1/100 cents. Limit one coupon per customer. Valid in the U.S. only.

5 65373 00076 2 (8100) 0 11556

SSECPNUS0808

Silhouette®

SPECIAL EDITION

HEART OF STONE
by
DIANA PALMER

On sale September.

SAVE $1.⁰⁰ OFF

**the Silhouette Special Edition® novel
HEART OF STONE on sale
September 2008, when you purchase
2 Silhouette Special Edition® books.**

*Available wherever books are sold, including most
bookstores, supermarkets, drugstores and discount stores.*

Coupon expires December 31, 2008. Redeemable at participating
retail outlets in Canada only. Limit one coupon per customer.

CANADIAN RETAILERS: Harlequin Enterprises Limited will pay the face value of this
coupon plus 10.25¢ if submitted by the customer for this specified product only. Any other
use constitutes fraud. Coupon is nonassignable. Void if taxed, prohibited or restricted by law.
Void if copied. Consumer must pay any government taxes. Nielsen Clearing House customers
("NCH") submit coupons and proof of sales to Harlequin Enterprises Limited, P.O. Box 3000,
Saint John, NB E2L 4L3, Canada. Non–NCH retailer: for reimbursement, submit coupons and
proof of sales directly to Harlequin Enterprises Limited, Retail Marketing Department, 225
Duncan Mill Rd., Don Mills (Toronto), ON M3B 3K9, Canada. Limit one coupon per purchase.
Valid in Canada only.

52608458

SSECPNCDN0808

REQUEST YOUR FREE BOOKS!
2 FREE NOVELS PLUS 2 FREE GIFTS!

SPECIAL EDITION®
Life, Love and Family!

YES! Please send me 2 FREE Silhouette Special Edition® novels and my 2 FREE gifts (gifts are worth about $10). After receiving them, if I don't wish to receive any more books, I can return the shipping statement marked "cancel." If I don't cancel, I will receive 6 brand-new novels every month and be billed just $4.24 per book in the U.S. or $4.99 per book in Canada, plus 25¢ shipping and handling per book and applicable taxes, if any*. That's a savings of at least 15% off the cover price! I understand that accepting the 2 free books and gifts places me under no obligation to buy anything. I can always return a shipment and cancel at any time. Even if I never buy another book from Silhouette, the two free books and gifts are mine to keep forever.

235 SDN EEYU   335 SDN EEY6

Name _____ (PLEASE PRINT) _____

Address _____ Apt. # _____

City _____ State/Prov. _____ Zip/Postal Code _____

Signature (if under 18, a parent or guardian must sign) _____

Mail to the **Silhouette Reader Service:**
IN U.S.A.: P.O. Box 1867, Buffalo, NY 14240-1867
IN CANADA: P.O. Box 609, Fort Erie, Ontario L2A 5X3

Not valid to current subscribers of Silhouette Special Edition books.

Want to try two free books from another line?
Call 1-800-873-8635 or visit www.morefreebooks.com.

* Terms and prices subject to change without notice. N.Y. residents add applicable sales tax. Canadian residents will be charged applicable provincial taxes and GST. Offer not valid in Quebec. This offer is limited to one order per household. All orders subject to approval. Credit or debit balances in a customer's account(s) may be offset by any other outstanding balance owed by or to the customer. Please allow 4 to 6 weeks for delivery. Offer available while quantities last.

Your Privacy: Silhouette is committed to protecting your privacy. Our Privacy Policy is available online at www.eHarlequin.com or upon request from the Reader Service. From time to time we make our lists of customers available to reputable third parties who may have a product or service of interest to you. If you would prefer we not share your name and address, please check here. ☐

SSE08R

NEW YORK TIMES BESTSELLING AUTHOR
SUSAN WIGGS

With her marriage in the rearview mirror, Sarah flees to her
hometown, a place she couldn't wait to leave. Now she finds
herself revisiting the past—a distant father and the unanswered
questions left by her mother's death. As she comes to terms with
her lost marriage, Sarah encounters a man she never expected to
meet again: Will Bonner, her high-school heartthrob. Now a local
firefighter, he's been through some changes himself. But just as her
heart opens, Sarah discovers she is pregnant—with her ex's twins.

It's hardly the most traditional of new beginnings, but who says life
or love are predictable...or perfect?

Just Breathe

"Susan Wiggs paints
the details of human
relationships with the
finesse of a master."
—*New York Times*
bestselling author
Jodi Picoult.

*Available the first
week of September 2008
wherever hardcovers
are sold!*

MIRA®

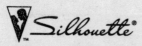

COMING NEXT MONTH

SSECNM0808